The Skin Of Our Teeth

PLAY IN THREE ACTS

By Thornton Wilder

SAMUEL FRENCH, INC.
45 West 25th Street   NEW YORK 10010
7623 Sunset Boulevard HOLLYWOOD 90046
LONDON   TORONTO

THE SKIN OF OUR TEETH

24 males; 11 females

STORY OF THE PLAY

Here is a comedy about George Antrobus, his wife and two children, and their general utility maid, Lily Sabina, all of Excelsior, New Jersey. George Antrobus is John Doe or George Spelvin or you—the average American at grips with a destiny, sometimes sour, sometimes sweet. The Antrobuses have survived fire, flood, pestilence, the seven-year locusts, the ice age, the black pox and the double feature, a dozen wars and as many depressions. They run many a gamut, are as durable as radiators, and look upon the future with a disarming optimism. Alternately bewitched, befuddled and becalmed, they are the stuff of which heroes are made—heroes and buffoons. They are true offspring of Adam and Eve, victims of all the ills that flesh is heir to. They have survived a thousand calamities by the skin of their teeth. Here is a tribute to their indestructibility.

3

SAMUEL FRENCH, INC.
can supply
the following
for use in productions of
THE SKIN OF OUR TEETH:

Sound effects cassette tape $32.50

Slides $14.50

PLUS POSTAGE

Copy of program of the first performance of "THE SKIN OF OUR TEETH" as given at the Plymouth Theatre in New York.

Michael Myerberg presents

Tallulah Bankhead   Fredric March
Florence Eldridge

in

THE SKIN OF OUR TEETH

A New Comedy

By Thornton Wilder

with a company of forty and
Florence Reed
Directed by Elia Kazan   Settings by Albert Johnson
Costumes by Mary Percy Schenck

ANNOUNCER	*Morton DaCosta*
SABINA	*Tallulah Bankhead*
MR. FITZPATRICK	*E. G. Marshall*
MRS. ANTROBUS	*Florence Eldridge*
DINOSAUR	*Remo Buffano*
MAMMOTH	*Andrew Ratousheff*
TELEGRAPH BOY	*Dickie Van Patten*
GLADYS	*Frances Heflin*
HENRY	*Montgomery Clift*
MR. ANTROBUS	*Fredric March*
DOCTOR	*Blair Davies*
PROFESSOR	*Ralph Kellard*
JUDGE	*Joseph Smiley*
HOMER	*Ralph Cullinan*
MISS E. MUSE	*Edith Faversham*
MISS T. MUSE	*Emily Lorraine*
MISS M. MUSE	*Eva Mudge Nelson*
USHER	*Stanley Prager*
USHER	*Harry Clark*
GIRL } *Drum Majorettes*	*Elizabeth Scott*
GIRL }	*Patricia Riordan*
FORTUNE TELLER	*Fiorence Reed*

5

CHAIR PUSHER .... *Earl Sydnor*
CHAIR PUSHER .... *Carroll Clark*
CONVEENER .... *Stanley Weede*
CONVEENER .... *Seumas Flynn*
CONVEENER .... *Aubrey Fassett*
CONVEENER .... *Stanley Prager*
CONVEENER .... *Harry Clark*
BROADCAST OFFICIAL .... *Morton DaCosta*
DEFEATED CANDIDATE .... *Joseph Smiley*
MR. TREMAYNE .... *Ralph Kellard*
HESTER .... *Eulabelle Moore*
IVY .... *Viole Dean*
FRED BAILEY .... *Stanley Prager*

ACT I. *Home, Excelsior, New Jersey.*

ACT II. *Atlantic City Boardwalk.*

ACT III. *Home, Excelsior, New Jersey.*

The Skin Of Our Teeth

ACT ONE

#1 Music—Overture, "William Tell Overture"

(SOUND CUE #1.)

A projection screen in the middle of a drop. The first lantern slide:
(#1 SLIDE—"News Events of the World." An An-
nouncer's voice is heard)
ANNOUNCER:
The management takes pleasure in bringing to you—
the news of the world:
(#2 SLIDE—The sun appearing above the hori-
zon.)
Freeport, Long Island.
The sun rose this morning at 6:32 a.m. This gratifying
event was first reported by
(#3 SLIDE)
Mrs. Dorothy Stetson of Freeport, Long Island, who
promptly telephoned the Mayor.
The Society for Affirming
(#4 SLIDE)
the End of the World at once went intto a special ses-
sion and postponed the arrival of that event for *twenty-*
four hours.
(#5 SLIDE)
All honor to Mrs. Stetson for her public spirit.
New York City:
(#6 SLIDE of the front doors of the theatre in
which this play is playing)
The Plymouth Theatre. During the daily cleaning of

this theatre a number of lost objects were collected, as usual

(#7 SLIDE)

by Mesdames Simpson, Pateslewski, and Moriarity.
Among these objects found today was

(#8 SLIDE)

a wedding ring, inscribed: To Eva from Adam. Genesis 2-18.
The ring will be restored to the owner or owners, if their credentials are satisfactory.
Tippehatchee, Vermont:

(#9 SLIDE)

The unprecedented cold weather of this summer has produced a condition that has not yet been satisfactorily explained. There is a report that a wall of ice is moving southward across these counties. The disruption of communications by the cold wave now crossing the country has rendered exact information difficult. Little credence is given to the rumor that the ice

(#10 SLIDE)

had pushed the Cathedral of Montreal as far as St. Albans, Vermont.
For further information see your daily papers.
Excelsior, New Jersey:

(#11 SLIDE of a modest suburban home)

The home of Mr. George Antrobus, the inventor of the wheel.
The discovery of the wheel, following so closely on the discovery of the lever, has centered the attention of the country on Mr. Antrobus of this attractive suburban residence district.
This is his home, a commodious seven-room house, conveniently situated near a public school, a Methodist church, and a fire-house; and it is right handy to an A. and P.

(#12 SLIDE of MR. ANTROBUS on his front steps, smiling and lifting his straw hat. He holds a wheel)

Mr. Antrobus, himself. He comes of very old stock and has made his way up from next to nothing.
It is reported that he was once a gardener, but left that

8   ACT I

situation under circumstances that have been variously reported.

Mr. Antrobus is a veteran of foreign wars, and bears a number of scars, front and back.

(#13 SLIDE of MRS. ANTROBUS, holding some roses)

This is Mrs. Antrobus, the charming and gracious president of the Excelsior Mothers' Club.

Mrs. Antrobus is an excellent needlewoman; it is she who invented the apron on which so many interesting changes have been wrung since that time.

(#14 SLIDE of the FAMILY and SABINA)

Here we see the Antrobuses with their two children, Henry and Gladys, and friend. The friend, in the rear, is Lily Sabina, the maid.

I know we all want to congratulate this typical American family on its enterprise.

(PROJECTION out. FLY CUE #1)

We all wish Mr. Antrobus a successful future. And now the management takes you to the interior of this home for a brief visit.

(LIGHT set up ½. PROPERTY CUE #1)

(Curtain rises. Living room of a commuter's home. There is enough open space between the lower ends of set, Right and Left, and the proscenium to show the fence that surrounds the house.

Down Right is a door to the kitchen and back yard; up Right is a pagoda with steps leading through and upstairs; up Center is a window; down Left is the front door.

A walnut Hamlet chair is below door Right; a backless bench up Right below pagoda; a sofa up Center below window; a lightweight round mahogany table Center; rocking chair Right of this table with hassock below the chair; armchair Left of table; two side tables above and below door Left; a clothes tree up Left corner; a pair of fire dogs down Center before an imaginary fireplace. SA-BINA — straw-blonde, over-rouged — enters from Right, crosses to the window back Center, on 6th

*chime, a feather duster under her elbow—looks
off Left, eyes shaded)*

SABINA:
Oh, oh, oh! Six o'clock and the master not home yet.
Pray God nothing serious has happened to him cross-
ing the Hudson River.
(To audience)
If anything happened to him, we would certainly be
inconsolable and have to move into a less desirable
residence district.
(Crossing to door Left)
The fact is I don't know what'll become of us. Here it
is the middle of August and the coldest day of the year.
(Looking through door window)
It's simply freezing; the dogs are sticking to the side-
walks;
(To audience)
can anybody explain that? No.
(Crossing to table down Left, dusting it)
But I'm not surprised. The whole world's at sixes and
sevens, and

(FLY CUE #2)

why the house hasn't fallen down about our ears long
ago is a miracle to me.
*(A fragment of the Left wall, flat "A," leans pre-
cariously over the stage. SABINA looks at it ner-
vously, backs away from it and it slowly rights
itself)*
Every night this same anxiety as to whether the master
will get home safely: whether he'll bring home anything to eat.
In the midst of life we are in the midst of death,
(Crosses to flat "A" to dust motto on wall)
a truer word was never said.

(FLY CUE #3)
*(The fragment of scenery, flat "B," flies up into
the lofts. SABINA is struck dumb with surprise,
shrugs shoulders and crosses to Left Center table
and starts dusting MR. ANTROBUS'S chair, including the under side)*

Of course, Mr. Antrobus is a very fine man, an excellent husband and father, a pillar of the church, and has all the best interests of the community at heart. Of course, every muscle goes tight every time he passes a policeman; but what I think is that there are certain charges that ought not to be made, and I think I may add, ought not to be allowed to be made; we're all human; who isn't?

(She crosses to chair Right of table, dusts Mrs.
Antrobus's *rocking chair, then stops dusting)*

Mrs. Antrobus is as fine a woman as you could hope to see. She lives only for her children; and if it would be any benefit to her children she'd see the rest of us stretched out dead at her feet without turning a hair—that's the truth.

(Dusts back of chair slightly)

If you want to know anything more about Mrs. Antrobus, just go and look at a tigress, and look hard.
As to the children—

(Crosses to above table Center—picks up slingshot from table)

Well, Henry Antrobus is a real, clean-cut American boy. He'll graduate from High School one of these days, if they make the alphabet any easier—

(Aims the slingshot)

Henry, when he has a stone in his hand, has a perfect aim; he can hit anything from a bird to an older brother—

(Slingshot down on table)

Oh! I didn't mean to say that!—but it certainly was an unfortunate accident, and it was very hard getting the Police out of the house.

(Crosses down Right Center to above hassock—dusts it)

Mr. and Mrs. Antrobus' daughter is named Gladys. She'll make some good man a good wife some day,

(To audience)

if he'll just come down off the movie screen and ask her.

So here we are!

(Crosses to fireplace down Center—dusts Right fire dog)

We've managed to survive for some time now, catch as catch can, the fat and the lean, and if the dinosaurs don't trample us to death, and if the grasshoppers don't eat up our garden, we'll all live to see better days, knock on wood.

(Knocks on wood. Crosses to Left fire dog—dusts it)

Each new child that's born to the Antrobuses seems to them to be sufficient reason for the whole universe's being set in motion; and each new child that dies seems to them to have been spared a whole world of sorrow, and what the end of it will be is still very much an open question.

(Crosses Right to dust picture on flat "B" above door Right)

We've rattled along,

(FLY CUE #4)

hot and cold, for some time now,

(To audience)

and my advice to you is not to inquire into why or whither, but just enjoy your ice cream while it's on your plate; that's my philosophy.

(Crosses down Right to chair—dusts it)

Don't forget that a few years ago we came through the depression by the skin of our teeth!

(Crosses to window)

One more tight squeeze like that and where will we be?

(This is a cue line. SABINA looks angrily at the Right door and repeats:)

—we came through the depression by the skin of our teeth; one more tight squeeze like that and where will we be?

(Flustered, she looks through the opening in the Left wall; then goes to the window and reopens the Act)

Oh, oh, oh! Six o'clock and the master not home yet.

(A quick look at door Right)

Pray God nothing has happened to him crossing the Hudson.

Here it is the middle of August and the coldest day of
the year. It's simply freezing; the dogs are sticking—
One more tight squeeze like that and where will we be?
FITZPATRICK:

>   (Off stage down Left)

Make up something! Invent something!
SABINA:

>   (Crossing down Left Center—polishing her nails
>   with duster)

Well—uh—this certainly is a fine American home—
and—uh—everybody's very happy—and—uh—

>   (Suddenly flings pretense to the winds and com-
>   ing downstage says with indignation:)

I can't invent any words for this play, and I'm glad I
can't.
I hate this play and every word in it.
As for me, I don't understand a single word of it, anyway,—all about the troubles the human race has gone
through, there's a subject for you.
Besides the author hasn't made up his silly mind as to
whether we're all living back in caves or in New Jersey, and that's the way it is all the way through.
Oh—why can't we have plays like we used to have—
Peg O' My Heart, and *Smilin' Thru,* and *The Bat,*
good entertainment with a message you can take home
with you?

>   (A quick look off Left)

I took this hateful job because I had to. For two years
I've sat up in my room living on a sandwich and a cup
of tea a day, waiting for better times in the theatre.

>   (Crosses to chair Left of table Center)

And look at me now: I—I who've played *Rain* and
The Barretts of Wimpole Street and *First Lady*—God!
FITZPATRICK:

>   (The stage manager puts his head out from the
>   proscenium down Left—points to door Right)

Miss Somerset!
SABINA:

>   (Sits chair Left of table)

Oh! Anyway—nothing matters! It'll all be the same in
a hundred years.

(Loudly)

Oh, oh, oh. We came through the depression by the skin of our teeth—that's true!—one more tight squeeze like that and where will we be?

(Enter MRS. ANTROBUS, from Right; a majestic matron carrying small watering can. Crosses to bulrushes on table down Left to water them)

MRS. ANTROBUS:
Sabina, you've let the fire go out.

SABINA:

(In a lather—puts duster on table—rises)

One-thing-and-another; don't-know-whether-my-wits-are-upside-or-down; might-as-well-be-dead-as-alive-in-a-house-all-sixes-and-sevens—

MRS. ANTROBUS:

(Turn to SABINA)

You've let the fire go out. Here it is the coldest day of the year right in the middle of August, and you've let the fire go out. *(Turns back to flowers.)*

SABINA:
Mrs. Antrobus, I'd like to give my two weeks' notice, Mrs. Antrobus. A girl like I can get a situation in a home where they're rich enough to have a fire in every room, Mrs. Antrobus, and a girl don't have to carry the responsibility of the whole house on her two shoulders.

(To Right of MRS. ANTROBUS)

And a home without children, Mrs. Antrobus, because children are a thing only a parent can stand, and a truer word was never said; and a home,

(MRS. ANTROBUS puts can under table)

Mrs. Antrobus, where the master of the house doesn't pinch decent, self-respecting girls when he meets them in a dark corridor.

(MRS. ANTROBUS turns to SABINA)

I mention no names and make no charges. So you have my notice, Mrs. Antrobus. I hope that's perfectly clear.

MRS. ANTROBUS.

(Crossing to table Center)

You've let the fire go out!—

(Turns to SABINA*)*

Have you milked the mammoth?

SABINA:

(To audience)

I don't understand a word of this play.—

(To MRS. ANTROBUS*)*

Yes, I've milked the mammoth.

MRS. ANTROBUS:

(Dusting paper scraps from table onto plate, moving to Right of table)

Until Mr. Antrobus comes home we have no food and we have no fire. You'd better go over to the neighbors and borrow some fire.

SABINA:

(Crossing to MRS. ANTROBUS*)*

Mrs. Antrobus! I can't! I'd die on the way, you know I would. It's worse than January. The dogs are sticking to the sidewalks. I'd die.

MRS. ANTROBUS:

Very well, I'll go.

SABINA:

(Even more distraught, coming forward and sinking on her knees)

You'd never come back alive; we'd all perish; if you weren't here, we'd just perish. How do we know Mr. Antrobus'll be back? We don't know. If you go out, I'll just kill myself.

MRS. ANTROBUS:

Get up, Sabina.

SABINA:

(Straightens up)

Every night it's the same thing. Will he come back safe, or won't he? Will we starve to death, or freeze to death, or boil to death or will we be killed by burglars?

(Sits chair Left of table)

I don't know why we go on living. I don't know why we go on living at all. It's easier being dead.

(She bursts into sobs, flings her arms on the arm of chair and buries her head in them. In each of the succeeding speeches she flings her head up—

*and sometimes her hands—then quickly buries her
head again.)*

MRS. ANTROBUS:
(Crossing to above chair Right of table)
The same thing! Always throwing up the sponge, Sabina. Always announcing your own death. But give you
a new hat—or a plate of ice cream—or a ticket to the
movies, and you want to live forever.

SABINA:
(Her head comes up)
You don't care whether we live or die; all you care is
about those children. If it would be any benefit to them
you'd be glad to see us all stretched out dead.

MRS. ANTROBUS:
Well, maybe I would.
*(Exits Right with plate of scraps and SABINA'S
duster.)*

SABINA:
(Rising)
And what do they care about? Themselves—that's all
they care about.
(Shrilly)
They make fun of you behind your back. Don't tell
me: they're ashamed of you. Half the time, they pre-
tend they're someone else's children. Little thanks you
get from them.

MRS. ANTROBUS:
*(Enters from Right carrying candlewick bed-
spread; crosses to Center)*
I'm not asking for any thanks.

SABINA:
And Mr. Antrobus—you don't understand *him*. All
that work he does—trying to discover the alphabet and
the multiplication table—whenever he tries to learn
anything you fight against it.

MRS. ANTROBUS:
Oh, Sabina, I know you.
When Mr. Antrobus raped you home from your
Sabine hills, he did it to insult me.
He did it for your pretty face and to insult me.
You were the new wife, weren't you?

16   ACT I

For a year or two you lay on your bed all day and polished the nails on your hands and feet:
You made puff-balls of the combings of your hair and you blew them up to the ceiling.
And I washed your underclothes and I made you chicken broths.
I bore children and between my very groans I stirred the cream that you'd put on your face.
But I knew you wouldn't last.
You didn't last.

(Hands SABINA one end of spread.)

SABINA:

(They fold spread lengthwise)

But it was I who encouraged Mr. Antrobus to make the alphabet.
I'm sorry to say it, Mrs. Antrobus, but you're not a beautiful woman,

(They meet face to face—fold spread in half)

and you can never know what a man could do if he tried.

(Fold in quarters)

It's girls like I who inspire the multiplication table.
I'm sorry to say it, but you're not a beautiful woman,

(They meet face to face—cover folded)

Mrs. Antrobus, and that's the God's truth.

MRS. ANTROBUS:

And you didn't last—you sank to the kitchen. And what do you do there? *You let the fire go out!*

(Takes cover—pushes SABINA into chair Left of table. Crossing up Center to sofa)

No wonder to you it seems easier being dead.
Reading and writing and counting on your fingers is all very well in their way—but I keep the home going.

(Puts cover on sofa—looks through window off Right)

—There's that dinosaur on the front lawn again.— Shoo! Go away. Go away.

(The baby DINOSAUR puts his head in the window.)

DINOSAUR:
It's cold.

MRS. ANTROBUS:
You go around to the back of the house where you
belong.

(FLY CUE #5)

*(She crosses Right, turns to window, watches the
DINOSAUR and MAMMOTH move across stage Left
to Right, then turns to audience. She joins their
laughter, then speaks to them and exits calmly
Right. The central portion of the back wall rises,
pauses, and disappears into the loft. SABINA
slowly raises her head.)*

SABINA:
Now that you audience are listening to this, too, I understand it a little better.
I wish eleven o'clock were here; I don't want to be
dragged through this whole play again.

*(The TELEGRAPH BOY is seen entering from the
Left. She catches sight of him, rises, and calls:)*

(LIGHT CUE #1)

Mrs. Antrobus! Mrs. Antrobus! Help! There's a
strange man coming to the house. He's coming up the
walk, help!

MRS. ANTROBUS:

*(Enters in alarm, but efficient, from Right. Crosses
Left. Gets the clothes tree and places it against
door Left)*

Help me quick!

*(TELEGRAPH BOY knocks at door. SABINA pushes
armchair from Left of table against base of
clothes tree. They barricade the door by piling the
furniture against it. MRS. ANTROBUS puts her
weight against chair. SABINA supports MRS. AN-
TROBUS from the rear)*

Who is it? What do you want?

*(DINOSAUR and MAMMOTH cross stage from Right
to Left to door Left.)*

TELEGRAPH BOY:
A telegram for Mrs. Antrobus from Mr. Antrobus in
the city.

SABINA:
Are you sure, are you sure? Maybe it's just a trap!
MRS. ANTROBUS:
(Turns to her)
I know his voice, Sabina. We can open the door.
(SABINA *pushes chair up Left and hides behind it.*
MRS. ANTROBUS *places tree up Left in corner, then
opens door. Enter the* TELEGRAPH BOY, *12 years
old, in uniform. The* DINOSAUR *and* MAMMOTH
*slip by him into the room and cross to fireplace
Center to warm themselves.* SABINA *and* TELE-
GRAPH BOY *carry on a flirtation.)*
I'm sorry we kept you waiting. We have to be careful,
you know.
(Crossing Center to the animals. DINOSAUR *moves
to Right of fireplace.* MAMMOTH *moves to Left of
fireplace.)*
Hm!—Will you be quiet?
(They nod)
Have you had your supper?
(They nod)
Are you ready to come in?
(They nod)
Young man, have you any fire with you?
(He nods)
Then light the grate, will you?
*(He nods, produces a kitchen match from his
pocket, goes to fireplace and kneels; lights match.
FOOTLIGHTS Center. Pause)*
                                    (LIGHT CUE #2)
What are people saying about this cold weather?
*(SABINA crosses Center to listen. He makes a
doubtful shrug of his shoulders.* SABINA *straight-
ens up)*
Sabina, take this stick and go and light the stove.
*(MRS. ANTROBUS hands her a twig, the end of
which is painted red, from fireplace.)*
SABINA:
(Takes stick; crossing to door Right)
Like I told you, Mrs. Antrobus; two weeks. That's
the law. I hope that's perfectly clear. *(Exits Right.)*

*(MAMMOTH lies down Left of fireplace—DINO-
SAUR crosses to above table Center, head on table
watching scene.)*

MRS. ANTROBUS:
(Sits chair Right of table)
What about this cold weather?
TELEGRAPH BOY:
(Crossing up to Left of table)
Of course, I don't know anything—but they say
there's a wall of ice moving down from the North,
that's what they say.
We can't get Boston by telegraph, and they're burning
pianos in Hartford.
It moves everything in front of it, churches and post
offices and city halls.
I live in Brooklyn myself.
MRS. ANTROBUS:
What are people doing about it?
TELEGRAPH BOY:
Well—uh— Talking, mostly.
Or just what you'd do a day in February.
There are some that are trying to go South and the
roads are crowded; but you can't take old people and
children very far in a cold like this.
MRS. ANTROBUS:
*(Pulls hassock to her; takes sewing basket from
table; puts it on hassock; darns a red sock)*
What's this telegram you have for me?
TELEGRAPH BOY:
(Fingertips to his forehead)
If you wait just a minute; I've got to remember it.
*(Steps Left Center, poses, arms folded, one foot
extended. The ANIMALS take places on either side
of him, leaning against his hips, like heraldic
beasts, the DINOSAUR to his Right, MAMMOTH to
his Left)*
This telegram was flashed from Murray Hill to Uni-
versity Heights! And then by puffs of smoke from
University Heights to Staten Island.

And then by lantern from Staten Island to Plainfield, New Jersey. What hath God wrought!

(He clears his throat)

"To Mrs. Antrobus, Excelsior, New Jersey:

My dear wife, will be an hour late. Busy day at the office. Don't worry the children about the cold just keep them warm. Burn everything except Shakespeare."

(Pause.)

MRS. ANTROBUS:

He knows I'd burn ten Shakespeares to prevent a child of mine from having one cold in the head. What does it say next?

(Enter SABINA Right to Right Center.)

TELEGRAPH BOY:

"Have made great discoveries today have separated em from en."

SABINA:

I know what that is, that's the alphabet, yes it is. Mr. Antrobus is just the cleverest man. Why, when the alphabet's finished, we'll be able to tell the future and everything.

TELEGRAPH BOY:

Then listen to this: "Ten tens make a hundred semicolon consequences far-reaching."

(Watches for effect.)

MRS. ANTROBUS:

The earth's turning to ice, and all he can do is to make up new numbers.

TELEGRAPH BOY:

Well, Mrs. Antrobus, like the head man at our office said: a few more discoveries like that and we'll be worth freezing.

MRS. ANTROBUS:

What does he say next?

TELEGRAPH BOY:

I—I can't do this last part very well.

(He clears his throat and sings to the tune of "Yankee Doodle")

"Happy w'dding ann'vers'ry to you, Happy ann'vers'ry to you—"

(The ANIMALS begin to howl soulfully; SABINA screams with pleasure.)

MRS. ANTROBUS:
Dolly! Frederick! Be quiet.

(DINOSAUR crosses up Left behind chair. MAMMOTH down Left—throws up his front feet—lies down.)

TELEGRAPH BOY:
(Drowned in the din)
"Happy w'dding ann'vers'ry, dear Eva; happy w'dding ann'vers'ry to you."

(SABINA looks admiringly at TELEGRAPH BOY.)

MRS. ANTROBUS:
Is that in the telegram? Are they singing telegrams now?
(He nods)
The earth's getting so silly no wonder the sun turns cold.
SABINA:
Mrs. Antrobus, I want to take back the notice I gave you.
Mrs. Antrobus, I don't want to leave a house that gets such interesting telegrams and I'm sorry for anything I said. I really am.
MRS. ANTROBUS:
Young man, I'd like to give you something for all this trouble; Mr. Antrobus isn't home yet and I have no money and no food in the house—
TELEGRAPH BOY:
Mrs. Antrobus—I don't like to—appear to—ask for anything, but—
MRS. ANTROBUS:
What is it you'd like?
TELEGRAPH BOY:
Do you happen to have an old needle you could spare? My wife just sits home all day thinking about needles.

SABINA:
> *(Shrilly)*

We only got two in the house. Mrs. Antrobus, you
know we only got two in the house.

MRS. ANTROBUS:
> *(After a look at* SABINA, *taking a needle from her*
> *collar, hands it to him)*

Why, yes, I can spare this.

TELEGRAPH BOY:
> *(Lowered eyes—takes needle)*

Thank you, Mrs. Antrobus. Mrs. Antrobus, can I ask
you something else? I have two sons of my own; if
the cold gets worse, what should I do?

SABINA:
I think we'll all perish, that's what I think. Cold like
this in August is just the end of the whole world.

> *(Silence.)*

MRS. ANTROBUS:
I don't know. After all, what does one do about anything? Just keep as warm as you can. And don't let
your wife and children see that you're worried.

TELEGRAPH BOY:
Yes. Thank you, Mrs. Antrobus. Well, I'd better be
going.

> (MRS. ANTROBUS *crosses to door Left)*

Oh, I forgot there's one more sentence in the telegram—

> *(Takes pose)*

"Three cheers have invented the wheel."

MRS. ANTROBUS:
A wheel? What's a wheel?

TELEGRAPH BOY:
I don't know. That's what it said. The sign for it is
like this.

> *(Gestures large circle)*

Well, goodbye.

> *(Looks at* SABINA, *clicks his tongue.)*

> (MRS. ANTROBUS *opens door for him as he exits.*

When door is opened ANIMALS *lower their heads to escape the cold.)*

SABINA:
  (Apron to her eyes, wailing)
Mrs. Antrobus, it looks to me like all the nice men in the world are already married;
  (Crossing Right to door)
I don't know why that is.
  (Sobs. Exits Right.)
MRS. ANTROBUS:
  (Thoughtful; to the ANIMALS*)*
Do you ever remember hearing of any cold like this in August?
  (The ANIMALS *shake their heads)*
From your grandmothers or anyone?
  (They shake their heads)
Have you any suggestions?
  *(*MAMMOTH *raises his front feet in doubt.* DINO-SAUR *wraps his arms around his body for warmth. She goes to the door Left and opening it an inch calls: the* ANIMALS *cross to window, huddle close together)*
Henry. Gladys. Children. Come right in and get warm.
No, no, when Mama says a thing she means it.
  *(*GLADYS *enters from down Left proscenium, crosses to door, running and laughing.* HENRY *follows)*
Henry! *Henry.* Put down that stone. You know what happened last time.
  *(*HENRY *gestures, throwing a rock when he reaches door)*
Henry!
  (Shriek. GLADYS *enters room, crosses down Right to chair, running)*
Put down that stone!
  *(*HENRY *throws again, then enters. Closes door.* MRS. ANTROBUS *crosses to Center)*
Gladys! Put down your dress!! Try and be a lady.

  (The CHILDREN *bound in and take off their win-*

*ter things and leave them in heaps on the chair
down Right and sofa up Center.)*

GLADYS:
*(Taking off coat, hat and gloves, places them on
chair down Right)*
Mama, I'm hungry. Mama, why is it so cold?
HENRY:
*(At the same time. Taking off jacket, sweater, hat,
gloves, places them on sofa)*
Mama, why doesn't it snow? Mama, when's supper
ready? Maybe it'll snow and we can make snowballs.
GLADYS:
Mama, it's so cold that in one more minute I couldn't
of stood it!
MRS. ANTROBUS:
Settle down, both of you, I want to talk to you.
*(She draws up a hassock and sits front Center
over the orchestra pit before the imaginary fire.
The CHILDREN stretch out on the floor, leaning
against her lap. Tableau of Raphael. The ANI-
MALS edge up and complete the triangle. MAM-
MOTH to GLADYS' Right. DINOSAUR to HENRY's
Left)*
It's just a cold spell of some kind. Now listen to what
I'm saying:
When your father comes home I want you to be extra
quiet. He's had a hard day at the office and I don't
know but what he may have one of his moods.
I just got a telegram from him very happy and ex-
cited, and you know what that means. Your father's
temper's uneven; I guess you know that.
(HENRY looks up at her. She shrieks)
Henry! Henry!
(Holds him by his hair)
Why—why can't you remember to keep your hair
down over your forehead?
*(HENRY covers his forehead with hand. MRS. AN-
TROBUS releases him. He pulls hair over scar)*
You must keep that scar covered up. Don't you know

that when your father sees it he loses all control over himself. He goes crazy. He wants to die?

(After a moment's despair she collects herself decisively, wets the hem of her apron in her mouth and starts polishing his forehead vigorously, holding him by the hair)

Lift your head up. Stop squirming. Blessed me, sometimes I think that it's going away—and then there it is: just as red as ever.

HENRY:

Mama, today at school two teachers forgot and called me by my old name. They forgot, Mama. You'd better write another letter to the principal, so that he'll tell them I've changed my name. Right out in class they called me: Cain.

MRS. ANTROBUS:

(Putting her hand on his mouth, too late; hoarsely)

Don't say it.

If you're good they'll forget it. Henry, you didn't—hurt anyone today, did you?

HENRY:

Oh—no-o-o!

(GLADYS fingers shame. HENRY gestures her away.)

MRS. ANTROBUS:

(Not looking at GLADYS)

And, Gladys, I want you to be especially nice to your father tonight. You know what he calls you when you're good—his little angel, his little star.

(Pulls down GLADYS' dress)

Keep your dress down like a little lady. And keep your voice nice and low. Gladys Antrobus!!! What's that red stuff

(GLADYS' hands go to her face)

you have on your face?

(Slaps her hand that she pulls from her face)

You're a filthy detestable child!

(Rises. Crosses Left to door. MAMMOTH moves

away to Right of chair Right Center. DINOSAUR
gets to his feet)

Get away from me, both of you! I wish I'd never seen
sight or sound of you. Let the cold come! I can't stand
it. I don't want to go on.
(She faces away from them.)

(DINOSAUR *edges close to* HENRY.)

GLADYS:
(Weeping—rises, crosses to above table)
All the girls at school do, Mama.
MRS. ANTROBUS:
(Shrieking)
I'm through with you, that's all!
(GLADYS *crosses Left toward* MRS. ANTROBUS.
HENRY *moves to Right of hassock facing them)*
—Sabina! Sabina!—Don't you know your father'd go
crazy if he saw that paint on your face? Don't you
know your father thinks you're perfect? Don't you
know he couldn't live if he didn't think you were per-
fect?—Sabina!
SABINA:
(Entering Right)
Yes, Mrs. Antrobus!
MRS. ANTROBUS:
Take this girl out into the kitchen and wash her face
with the scrubbing brush.

(GLADYS *starts Right, but stops on noise.)*

ANTROBUS:
(Outside, roaring)
Look out below!!
(Singing)
"I've been working on the railroad, all the livelong
day—" etc.

(The ANIMALS *try to hide.* DINOSAUR *under table,*
MAMMOTH *behind chair Right Center.* SABINA
tries to hide alongside MAMMOTH. HENRY *rises,*
crosses Right Center, watching.)

MRS. ANTROBUS:
Sabina, what's that noise outside?
SABINA:
(Crossing above table to Left of it)
Oh, it's a drunken tramp. It's a giant, Mrs. Antrobus.
We'll all be killed in our beds, I know it!
MRS. ANTROBUS:
Help me quick. Quick.
(ANTROBUS enters around fence Left, crosses to door Left, singing. Again they stack the tree and chair against the door. MRS. ANTROBUS, GLADYS, SABINA help block door by pushing against chair)
Who is it? What do you want?—Sabina, have you any boiling water ready?—Who is it?

(HENRY picks up slingshot from table, steps back to take aim.)

ANTROBUS:
Broken-down camel of a pig's snout, open this door.
MRS. ANTROBUS:
God be praised! It's your father.—Just a minute!
George, Sabina, clear the door, quick.
(Taking GLADYS to Center)
Gladys, come here while I clean your nasty face!

(SABINA places tree and chair up Left.)

ANTROBUS:
She-bitch of a goat's gizzard, I'll break every bone in your body. Let me in or I'll tear the whole house down.
MRS. ANTROBUS:
Just a minute, George, something's the matter with the lock.

(SABINA stands at door, fingers in ears, awaiting orders.)

ANTROBUS:
Open the door or I'll turn your livers out. I'll smash your brains on the ceiling, and the devil take the hindmost.

28   ACT I

MRS. ANTROBUS:
Now I'm ready, Sabina. You can open the door.

> (MRS. ANTROBUS *pushes hassock to Right Cen-*
> *ter.* SABINA *opens door—closes it after* ANTROBUS
> *enters. The door is flung open. Silence.* ANTROBUS
> *enters, face of a Keystone Comedy Cop—stands*
> *there in fur cap and blanket. His arms are full of*
> *parcels, including a large stone wheel with a cen-*
> *ter in it. One hand carries a railroad man's lan-*
> *tern. Suddenly he bursts into joyous roar)*

ANTROBUS:
Well, how's the whole crooked family?
> *(Relief. Laughter. Tears. Jumping up and down.*
> ANIMALS *cavorting.* ANTROBUS *throws the parcels*
> *on the ground. Heroic embraces. Melee of hu-*
> *mans and animals,* SABINA *included. He holds*
> GLADYS *in his Left arm.* GLADYS *unwraps his*
> *scarf)*

I'll be scalded and tarred if a man can't get a little wel-
come when he comes home.
> (SABINA *takes his hat and gloves)*

Well, Maggie, you old gunny-sack, how's the broken
down old weather hen—Sabina, old fishbait, old skunk-
pot.—And the children,—how've the little smellers
been?
GLADYS:
> *(Hanging on to him)*

Papa, Papa, Papa, Papa, Papa.

> (SABINA *takes his scarf.)*

ANTROBUS:
How've they been, Maggie? How've they been?
MRS. ANTROBUS:
Well, I must say, they've been as good as gold. I
haven't had to raise my voice once.

> (HENRY *crosses Left to him and takes wheel, then*
> *starts Right above table.* SABINA *takes his blanket.)*

ANTROBUS:
(Holding GLADYS)
Papa's little weasel, eh? Sabina, there's some food for you.
(Indicates to parcels on floor)
Papa's little gopher?

(SABINA bends over to pick up parcels and shopping bag.)

GLADYS:
(Her arms around his neck)
Papa, you're always teasing me.
ANTROBUS:
And Henry?
(HENRY stops up Center)
Nothing rash today, I hope. Nothing rash?
HENRY:
No, Papa.
(Crosses to bench up Right, sits, examines wheel.)
ANTROBUS:
(Roaring)
Well, that's good, that's good—I'll bet Sabina let the fire go out.
(He slaps SABINA's backside as she is bent over. She straightens up sharply.)
SABINA:
Mr. Antrobus, I've given my notice. I'm leaving two weeks from today. I'm sorry, but I'm leaving.
(To door Right.)
ANTROBUS:
(Roar)
Well, if you leave now you'll freeze to death, so go and cook the dinner.
SABINA:
(Takes lantern from his Left arm and puts it on floor under table down Left)
Two weeks, that's the law.
(Gesture of pain where she was slapped. Exits Right with clothes and parcels)

(DINOSAUR crosses to ANTROBUS with large bone

in his mouth. ANTROBUS *takes it and throws it against door Right.* DINOSAUR *chases it and pounces on it.)*

ANTROBUS:
   (Crosses Center to MRS. ANTROBUS *by the fire)*
Did you get my telegram?
   (A quick kiss on her cheek.)
MRS. ANTROBUS:
Yes.—What's a wheel?
ANTROBUS:
Why, there it is—
   (He indicates the wheel with a glance. HENRY *is examining it. She catches his arm and pulls him to fireplace. Rapid, hoarse interchange:)*
MRS. ANTROBUS:
What does this cold weather mean? It's below freezing.
ANTROBUS:
Not before the children!
MRS. ANTROBUS:
Shouldn't we do something about it?—start off, move?
ANTROBUS:
Not before the children!!!
   (He crosses to and gives HENRY *a sharp slap.)*

   *(*GLADYS *goes to Left of* MRS. ANTROBUS. HENRY *down to Right of* ANTROBUS.)*

HENRY:
Papa, you hit me!
ANTROBUS:
Well, remember it.
   *(*DINOSAUR *goes up Right with bone)*
That's to make you remember today. Today. The day the alphabet's finished; and the day that we *saw* the hundred—the hundred, the hundred, the hundred, the hundred, the hundred—there's no end to 'em. I've had a day at the office! By the way, Maggie.
   (Takes wheels from HENRY)
Take a look at that wheel, Maggie—when I've got that to rights: you'll see a sight.

(He rolls wheel to Left front of Mrs. Antrobus. Gladys, *giggling, backs away as it comes
toward her)*
There's a reward there for all the walking you've done.

*(*Dinosaur *crosses up to window.)*

Mrs. Antrobus:
How do you mean?
Antrobus:
(Holding the wheel. With awe)
Maggie—we've reached the top of the wave. There's
not much left to be done. We're there!
Mrs. Antrobus:
And the ice???
Antrobus:
The ice!

(He rolls the wheel Right to Henry, *who catches
it. The wheel comes so close to* Mrs. Antrobus
her leg goes up in the air to avoid it.)

Mrs. Antrobus:
Children, go out in the kitchen. I want to talk to your
father alone.

(Crossing to get Gladys, *who has just taken* Antrobus' *coat off.* Antrobus *goes to chair up Left,
sits and takes off overshoes.* Mrs. Antrobus *and*
Gladys *cross to door Right.)*

Henry:
Papa, you could put a chair on this.
Antrobus:
Yes, any booby can fool with it now; but I thought of
it first.

*(*Dinosaur *crosses to Right of chair.* Mammoth
crosses to Left of chair. Exit Gladys *and* Henry
Right. Antrobus *in his chair up Left. He takes
the goldfish bowl on his lap; pulls the canary cage*

ACT I

THE SKIN OF OUR TEETH

Act I, See Page 32

THE SKIN OF OUR TEETH

Act II, See Page 56

down to the level of his face. Both the ANIMALS
put their paws up on the arm of his chair. MRS.
ANTROBUS *faces him across the room, like
judge.)*

(LIGHT CUE #3)

MRS. ANTROBUS:
Well?
ANTROBUS:
(Shortly)
It's cold.—
(To fish)
How things been, eh? Keck, keck, keck.—
(To bird)
And you, Millicent?
MRS. ANTROBUS:
I know it's cold.
ANTROBUS:
(To the bird)
No spilling of sunflower seed, eh? No singing after
lights-out, y'know what I mean?
MRS. ANTROBUS:
You can try and prevent us freezing to death, can't
you? You can do something? We can start moving. Or
we can go on the animals' backs?
ANTROBUS:
The best thing about animals is that they don't talk
much.
DINOSAUR:
(Quick cue)
It's cold.
MAMMOTH:
It's cold.
ANTROBUS:
Eh, eh, eh! Watch that!—
*(*MAMMOTH *crosses down Left. Lies down.)*
—By midnight we'd turn to ice. The roads are full of
people now who can scarcely lift a foot from the
ground. The grass out in front is like iron,—which re-
minds me, I have another needle for you.
(Turns his coat lapel to show her)

ACT I   33

—The people up north—where are they? Frozen—crushed—

MRS. ANTROBUS:
Is that what's going to happen to us?
(ANTROBUS whistles to bird)
Will you answer me?

ANTROBUS:
I don't know, Maggie. I don't know anything. Some say that the ice is going slower.
(Puts fish bowl on table up Left)
Some say that it's stopped. The sun's growing cold. What can I do about that? Nothing we can do but burn everything in the house, and the fenceposts and the barn. Keep the fire going.
(Rises; a step down Left)
When we have no more fire, we die.

(JUDGE enters from up Left. Crosses around fence to window. DOCTOR and MISS E. MUSE enter from up Left; cross around fence to door Left.)

MRS. ANTROBUS:
Well, why didn't you say so in the first place?

(She is about to march off into the kitchen, when two REFUGEES, men, appear against the back wall, soon joined by OTHERS. They are heard calling.)

MISS T. MUSE:
(From up Right)
Mr. Antrobus.   *(LIGHT CUE #4.)*

JUDGE:
(From up Center)
Mr. Antrobus.

HOMER:
(From up Right)
Mr. Antrobus.

MRS. ANTROBUS:
Who's that? Who's that calling you?

ANTROBUS:
(Clears his throat)
Hm—let me see.
(He turns to Left door.)

34   ACT I

(THREE REFUGEES are at the window—OTHERS stand farther off.)

JUDGE:
Could we warm our hands for a moment, Mr. Antrobus?

MISS T. MUSE:
It's very cold, Mr. Antrobus.

HOMER:
Mr. Antrobus, I wonder if you have a piece of bread or something you could spare?

(Silence—they wait humbly. MRS. ANTROBUS stands rooted to the spot. Suddenly a KNOCKING at the door Left, then KNOCKING at the door Right, then KNOCKING at both doors— short rapid blows.)

MRS. ANTROBUS:
Who are these people? Why, they are all over the front yard. What did they come here for?

(SABINA enters from Right. KNOCKING ceases.)

SABINA:
Mrs. Antrobus, there are thousands of tramps knocking at the back door.

MRS. ANTROBUS:
George, tell these people to go away. Tell them to move right along. I'll go and send them away from the back door. Sabina, come with me.
(She goes out Right energetically.)

ANTROBUS:
Sabina, stay here. I have something to say to you.
(He goes to door Left, opens it a crack and talks through it. SABINA crosses to him, stands back of him at door)
Ladies and Gentlemen—I'll have to ask you to wait a few minutes longer. It'll be all right. While you're waiting, you might each pull up a stake of the fence. We'll need them all for the fireplace. There'll be coffee and sandwiches in a moment.

SABINA:

    (Suddenly extends her arm, pointing through the window of the door with a scream)

Mr. Antrobus, what's that? What's that big white thing moving this way? Mr. Antrobus, it's ice—it's ice.

ANTROBUS:

    (Pushing her to Center)

Sabina, I want you to go into the kitchen and make a lot of coffee. Make a whole pailful.

SABINA:

Pailful?

ANTROBUS:

    (With gesture)

And sandwiches, piles of them, like this.

SABINA:

Mr. An—

    (Suddenly she drops the play, and says in her own person as Miss Somerset, with surprise)

Oh, I see what this part of the play means now. This means refugees.

    (She steps away from him and says:)

Oh, I don't like it—I don't like it.

    (She crosses down to the footlights and energetically says to the audience:)

Ladies and Gentlemen, don't take this play serious. The world's not coming to an end—you know it's not. People exaggerate. Most people really have enough to eat and a roof over their heads. Nobody actually starves—you can always eat grass or something—that ice business—why, it was a long, long time ago.

ANTROBUS: } *(Together)*
FITZPATRICK

    (From down Left proscenium)

Miss Somerset!

Miss Somerset!

SABINA:

All right, I'll say the lines, but I won't think about the play. And I advise you not to think about the play either.   *(Exits Right below the set.)*

    (MRS. ANTROBUS *enters from door Right, crosses*

*to door Left and stands guard there. KNOCKING
is heard at door Left.)*

MISS M. MUSE:
(Calling from up Right)
Mr. Antrobus—Mr. Antrobus.
MRS. ANTROBUS:
George, these tramps say that you asked them to come
to the house. What does this mean?

*(KNOCKING stops. DOCTOR crosses up Center to
outside window.)*

ANTROBUS:
Just—they're a few friends I met on the road.
MRS. ANTROBUS:
Now you're not to let these people in.
ANTROBUS:
They're real nice—real useful people—
MRS. ANTROBUS:
(Back to door)
George Antrobus, not another soul comes in here over
my dead body.
ANTROBUS:
(Crossing to her)
Maggie, there's a doctor there.
(DOCTOR looks in through window)
Never hurts to have a good doctor in the house. We've
lost a peck of children, one way and another. You can
never tell when a child's throat will get stopped up.
What you and I have seen—!!!
*(He puts his fingers on his throat, and imitates
diphtheria.)*
MRS. ANTROBUS:
Well, just one person, then, the doctor.
*(Pushes chair from up Left to Left of table Cen-
ter)*
The others can go right along the road.
ANTROBUS:
Maggie, there's an old man, particular friend of
mine—

ACT I   37

MRS. ANTROBUS:
I won't listen to you—
ANTROBUS:
It was he that really started off the A.B.C.'s.
MRS. ANTROBUS:
I don't care if he perishes. We can do without reading or writing. We can't do without food.

(MISS M. MUSE *joins group at window.*)

ANTROBUS:
Then let the ice come!!
    (Crossing Right to hassock)
Drink your coffee!! I don't want any coffee if I can't drink it with some good people.
    (Sits hassock.)
MRS. ANTROBUS:
Stop shouting. Who else is there trying to push us off the cliff?
ANTROBUS:
Well, there's the man—who makes all the laws. Judge Moses.

(JUDGE *looks in through window.* MISS E. MUSE *joins group at window.*)

MRS. ANTROBUS:
    (Crossing to look out window)
Judges can't help us now.
ANTROBUS:
And if the ice melts?—and if we pull through? Have you and I been able to bring up Henry?
    (MRS. ANTROBUS *looks at him*)
What have we done?
MRS. ANTROBUS:
Who are those old women?
ANTROBUS:
    (Coughs)
Up in town there are nine sisters. There are three or four of them here. They're sort of music teachers— and one of them recites and one of them—

MRS. ANTROBUS:
That's the end A singing troupe!
(Crossing down Left)
Well, take your choice, live or die. Starve your own
children before your face.
ANTROBUS.
(Gently. Rising, crossing to her)
These people don't take much. They're used to starving.
They'll sleep on the floor.
Besides, Maggie, listen!
(She turns away)
No, listen:
Who've we got in the house but Sabina? Sabina's al-
ways afraid the worst will happen. Whose spirits can
she keep up? Maggie, these people never give up. They
think they'll live and work forever.
MRS. ANTROBUS:
(Walks slowly to Right Center)
All right, let them in.
(ANTROBUS *starts for door Left*)
You're master here.
(Softly)
—But these animals must go.
(He stops at door. MAMMOTH rises)
Enough's enough. They'll soon be big enough to push
the walls down, anyway.
(MAMMOTH *backs away*)
Take them away.
(Crosses to Right Center.)
ANTROBUS:
(Sadly)
All right. The dinosaur and mammoth—! Come on
baby, come on, Frederick. Come for a walk. That's ს
good little Fellow.

(MAMMOTH *crosses to door slowly, turns and
looks at* ANTROBUS. DINOSAUR *crosses to Right of*
ANTROBUS *with bone in mouth. He growls at*
MAMMOTH, *who exits.* DINOSAUR *indicates bone.*
ANTROBUS *takes it from him.)*

DINOSAUR:
It's cold.
ANTROBUS:
Yes, nice cold fresh air.
          (*Pats animals on back with bone*)
Bracing.
          (DINOSAUR *exits running*)
          (*He holds the door open as the* ANIMALS *go out.
          He puts bone on floor down Left. He beckons to
          his friends. The seedy* CROWD *shuffles in.* ANTRO-
          BUS *introduces them, confusedly mumbling to*
          MRS. ANTROBUS, *who bows with a stately bend of
          the head*)
Make yourself at home. Maggie, this the doctor—m—
          (DOCTOR *crosses to up Left corner. Puts hat and
          ba: down*)
Professor, this is my wife—
          (PROFESSOR *crosses down Left; carries bag of
          books*)
And—Judge—Maggie, you know the Judge.
          (JUDGE *hesitates*)
Come right in, Judge.
          (JUDGE *crosses up Center*)
Coffee'll be here in a minute.
          (*The old* BLIND MAN *with a guitar is* HOMER)
Maggie, you know—you know Homer?
          (MRS. ANTROBUS *crosses down Right; picks up*
          GLADYS' *clothes from chair*)
—Professor, will you—
          (*He leads* HOMER *to the* PROFESSOR)
Miss Muse—are some of your sisters here? Come right
in— Miss E. Muse; Miss T. Muse; Miss M. Muse.

          (*The* MUSES *huddle together Left Center.*)

MRS. ANTROBUS:
How do you do? Pleased to meet you.
Just—make yourself comfortable. Supper'll be ready
in a minute. ·

          (*She goes out Right abruptly.* ANTROBUS *crosses*

Right to her, but she has gone. He then turns to the GUESTS.)

ANTROBUS:

Maggie—! Make yourself at home, friends.

(The GUESTS *quickly move about the room.* MISS T. MUSE *to Right of table Center.* MISS M. MUSE *to down Right Center.* MISS E. MUSE *above table to up Right.* PROFESSOR *leads* HOMER *to chair Left of table, seats him, then crosses up to sofa.* JUDGE *and* DOCTOR *down Left.* ANTROBUS *above table Center; places sewing basket on floor. Enter* SABINA *and* MRS. ANTROBUS, *bearing two platters of sandwiches, trays of coffee, mugs and spoons.* SABINA *stops and stares at* REFUGEES, *between* MISS T. *and* MISS M. MUSE. MRS. ANTROBUS *to above table and places cups on table.)*

Sabina, pass the sandwiches.

SABINA:

I thought I was working in a respectable house—that had respectable guests. I'm giving my notice, Mr. Antrobus, two weeks, that's the law.

ANTROBUS:

Booby, pass the sandwiches.

SABINA:

Two weeks, that's the law.

(Crosses to table; places sandwiches, trays on table.)

ANTROBUS:

(Indicates JUDGE)

There's the law. That's Moses.

SABINA:

(Stares)

The Ten Commandments— *Faugh!!—*

(To audience)

That's the worst line I've ever had to say on any stage.

(Exits Right.)

ANTROBUS:

I think the best thing to do is just not to stand on ceremony, but pass the sandwiches around from right to left. Judge, help yourself to one of these.

(MISS T. MUSE *takes sandwich tray; sits hassock.*
MISS E. MUSE *takes sandwich, then moves back
up Right.* MISS M. MUSE *takes tray from* MISS T.
MUSE. JUDGE *takes tray from* ANTROBUS; *takes
sandwich.* PROFESSOR *takes two sandwiches; gives
one to* HOMER. DOCTOR *takes tray from* JUDGE.
ANTROBUS *hands two cups to* PROFESSOR; *takes
two more cups; gives one to* HOMER; *keeps one
for self.)*

MRS. ANTROBUS:
(Serving cup to MISS E. MUSE*)*
The roads are crowded, I hear?

(*The* GUESTS *all talking at once:)*

MISS E. MUSE:
People are trampling one another.
DOCTOR:
Ma'am, you can't imagine.
MISS M. MUSE:
You can hardly put one foot before you.

(Sudden silence. MISS M. MUSE *puts sandwich
tray on chair down Right.* DOCTOR *puts sandwich
tray on table down Left.)*

MRS. ANTROBUS:
(Serving cup to MISS T. MUSE*)*
Well, you know what I think it is,—I think it's sun-
spots!
(Crosses to above table Center.)

(*The* GUESTS, *discreet hubbub:)*

HOMER:
Oh, you're right, Mrs. Antrobus—
THE MUSES:
That's what it is—
JUDGE:
That's what I was saying the other day.

(Sudden silence)

(MRS. ANTROBUS *serves cup to* MISS M. MUSE, *then crosses to table for cup for self.*)

ANTROBUS:
(Crossing to JUDGE *Left Center)*
Well, I don't believe the whole world's going to turn to ice.
(All eyes are fixed on him, waiting)
I can't believe it. Judge! Have we worked for nothing? Professor! Have we just failed in the whole thing?
MRS. ANTROBUS:
(Crossing to chair Right of table)
It is certainly very strange—well on both sides of the family we come of very hearty stock.
(Sits chair)
—Doctor, I want you to meet my children. They're eating their supper now. And of course I want them to meet you.
DOCTOR.
Of course!
MISS M. MUSE:
How many children have you, Mrs. Antrobus?
MRS. ANTROBUS:
I have two,—a boy and a girl.
JUDGE:
(Softly)
I understood you had two sons, Mrs. Antrobus.

(All GUESTS *look sharply at* JUDGE.)

MRS. ANTROBUS:
(Rises in blind suffering; then sits again; then rises and walks toward the footlights. In a low voice)
Abel, Abel, my son, my son, Abel, my son,
(The GUESTS *move with few steps toward her as though in comfort, murmuring words in Greek, Hebrew, German, etcetera.)*
Abel, my son.

*(A piercing shiek from the kitchen—*SABINA'S

voice. All heads turn. GUESTS *back away.* HOMER
rises. PROFESSOR *helps him up Center.)*

ANTROBUS:
*(Crosses to table; leaves cup, then to down front
of chair Left of table)*
What's that?

*(*SABINA *enters; crosses to Right of* MRS. ANTRO-
BUS, *bursting with indignation.* GLADYS *follows*
SABINA *in; crosses to above door Right.)*

SABINA:
Mr. Antrobus—that son of yours, that boy Henry Antrobus— I don't stay in this house another moment!—
He's not fit to live among respectable folks and that's
a fact.

MRS. ANTROBUS:
Don't say another word, Sabina. I'll be right back.
*(Without waiting for an answer she goes past her
into the kitchen.)*

*(*MISS M. MUSE *joins other two up Right.)*

SABINA:
Mr. Antrobus, Henry has thrown a stone again and if
he hasn't killed the boy that lives next door, I'm very
much mistaken. He finished his supper and went out to
play; and I heard such a fight; and then I saw it. I
saw it with my own eyes. And it looked to me like stark
murder.

*(*MRS. ANTROBUS *appears at the kitchen door,
shielding* HENRY, *who follows her. When she
steps aside, we see on* HENRY'S *forehead a large
ochre and scarlet scar in the shape of a C.* ANTRO-
BUS *makes a start for him.* MRS. ANTROBUS *steps
to* HENRY *to shield him. A pause.)*

HENRY:
*(Below door Right, is heard saying under his
breath:)*

He was going to take the wheel away from me. He
started to throw a stone at me first.

MRS. ANTROBUS:

George, it was just a boyish impulse. Remember how
young he is.

(Louder, in an urgent wail)

George, he's only four thousand years old.

SABINA:

And everything was going along so nicely!

(Silence.)

ANTROBUS:

Put out the fire!

*(Crosses to fireplace. He starts stamping out the
fire)*

Put out all the fires.

(Violently)   (*LIGHT CUE #5.*)

No wonder the sun grows cold.

MRS. ANTROBUS:

Doctor! Judge! Help me!

(They step toward him)

—George,

*(Crosses to him. SABINA crosses to Right of MRS.
ANTROBUS)*

have you lost your mind?

ANTROBUS:

There is no mind. We'll not try to live.

*(To the GUESTS up Left, crossing up toward
them)*

Give it up. Give up trying.

*(JUDGE, PROFESSOR and DOCTOR step up Left;
huddle together, arms folded. MRS. ANTROBUS sits
in chair Left of table, head in hands.)*

SABINA:

Mr. Antrobus! I'm downright ashamed of you.

MRS. ANTROBUS:

George, have some more coffee. Gladys! Where's
Gladys gone?

(SABINA crosses Right to GLADYS. GLADYS steps in, frightened.)

GLADYS:

Here I am, Mama.

MRS. ANTROBUS:

Go upstairs and bring your father's slippers.

(GLADYS starts for stairs)

How could you forget a thing like that, when you know how tired he is?

(He covers his face with his hands. GLADYS exits up stairs. MRS. ANTROBUS turns to the REFUGEES:)

Can't some of you sing? It's your business in life to sing, isn't it?

(THREE MUSES sit bench up Right)

Sabina!

(SABINA starts "Jingle Bells." They start singing: "Jingle Bells"; later MRS. ANTROBUS continues to ANTROBUS in a low voice, singing quieter)

George, remember all the other times. When the volcanoes came right up in the front yard.

(Crossing to him and taking off his shoes)

And the time the grasshoppers ate every single leaf and blade of grass, and all the grain and spinach you'd grown with your own hands. And the summer there were earthquakes every night.

ANTROBUS:

Henry! Henry!

(HENRY crosses up Center above table; puts his hand on his forehead)

Myself. All of us, we're covered with blood.

MRS. ANTROBUS:

Then remember all the times you were pleased with him and when you were proud of yourself.

(Rises)

—Henry!

HENRY:

Yes, Mama. *(Crosses to Left of ANTROBUS.)*

MRS. ANTROBUS:

Henry! Come here and recite to your father the multiplication table that you do so nicely.

46

(GLADYS enters from stairs with slippers; comes to Right of MRS. ANTROBUS. MRS. ANTROBUS makes stern pantomime gesture to GLADYS: Go in there and do your best. Singing stops. HENRY kneels on one knee beside his father and starts whispering the multiplication table.)

HENRY:
(Finally—kneeling)
Two times six is twelve; three times six is eighteen—
I don't think I know the sixes.

(The GUESTS are now singing "Tenting Tonight.")

GLADYS:
(Crossing to his Right—puts on slippers)
Papa—Papa—I was very good in school today. Miss Conover said right out in class that if all the girls had as good manners as Gladys Antrobus, that the world would be a very different place to live in.

MRS. ANTROBUS:
You recited a piece at assembly, didn't you?
(Fierce glance at GLADYS)
Recite it to your father.

GLADYS:
Papa, do you want to hear what I recited in class?
(Singing stops)
"The Star," by Henry Wadsworth Longfellow.

MRS. ANTROBUS:
Wait!!!
(Crossing down to fireplace)
The fire's going out.
(Singing starts, "Jingle Bells")
There isn't enough wood! Henry, go upstairs and bring down the chairs
(HENRY crosses up Right to stairs)
and start breaking up the beds.

(Exit HENRY up stairs. Singing quieter.)

GLADYS:
Look, Papa, here's my report card. Lookit. Conduct A!

Look, Papa. Papa, do you want to hear "The Star," by Henry Wadsworth Longfellow? Papa, you're not mad at me, are you?—I know it'll get warmer. Soon it'll be just like Spring, and we can go to a picnic at the Hibernian Picnic Grounds like you always like to do, don't you remember? Papa, just look at me once.

(Her head on his knee.)

(Singing stops. Enter HENRY *with some chairs he holds on step.)*

ANTROBUS:
(Pause. ANTROBUS *lifts her head; looks at her)*
You recited in assembly, did you?
(She nods eagerly)
You didn't forget it?
GLADYS:
No!!! I was perfect.

*(*ANTROBUS *looks up at* MRS. ANTROBUS. *Pause. Then* ANTROBUS *rises; goes to the door Left; the* GUESTS *draw back timidly; he peers out of the door at the ice.)*

ANTROBUS:
(With decision, suddenly closes door; crosses to fireplace. HENRY *crosses down Center; places chair pieces in fire)*
Build up the fire. It's cold. Build up the fire. We'll do what we can. Sabina, get more wood.
(She exits Right)
Come around the fire, everybody. Bring up your benches.
*(*JUDGE *and* PROFESSOR *carry sofa to Left Center.* MUSES *carry bench to Right Center.* MRS. ANTROBUS *sits chair Right of table)*
At least the young ones may pull through.
(Pulling HENRY *to his Left)*
Henry, have you eaten something?
HENRY:
Yes, Papa.   *(LIGHT CUE #6)*

ANTROBUS:
Gladys, have you had some supper?
GLADYS:
I ate in the kitchen, Papa.
ANTROBUS:
(Sits chair Left of table Center, holding GLADYS'
and HENRY'S *hands)*
If you do come through this—what'll you be able to do?
What do you know? Henry, did you take a good look
at that wheel?
HENRY:
Yes, Papa.
ANTROBUS:
Six times two are—
HENRY:
—twelve; six times three are eighteen; six times four
are— Papa, it's hot and cold. It makes my head all
funny. It makes me sleepy.
ANTROBUS:
(Gives him a cuff)
Wake up. I don't care if your head is sleepy. Six times
four are twenty-four. Six times five are—
HENRY:
Thirty. Papa!   *(WARN Curtain.)*
ANTROBUS:
Maggie, put something into Gladys' head on the chance
she can use it.
MRS. ANTROBUS:
What should it be, George?
ANTROBUS:
Six times six are thirty-six.
Teach her the beginning of the Bible.
GLADYS:
But, Mama, it's so cold and close.

*(*MRS. ANTROBUS *pulls* GLADYS *to her Right.*
HENRY *has all but drowsed off. His father slaps
him sharply and the lesson goes on.)*

MRS. ANTROBUS: *(LIGHT CUE #7)*
"In the beginning God created the heavens and the
earth;

*(Gladys repeats each phrase. Antrobus continues
with the table. Henry repeats after him. Sabina
enters from Right with pieces of furniture)*
and the earth was waste and void; and the darkness
was upon the face of the deep—"

(The singing starts up again louder.)

Sabina:
*(Coming down to the footlights, tossing wood in
fireplace)*
Will you please start handing up your chairs? We'll
need everything for this fire. Save the human race.—
Ushers, will you pass the chairs up here?
Thank you.

(Singing starts—"Jingle Bells"—Guests.)

Henry:
Six times nine are fifty-four; six times ten are sixty.
                    (PROPERTY CUE #2)
*(In the back of the auditorium the sound of chairs
being ripped up can be heard. An Usher rushes
down the aisle with chairs and hands them over.
Sabina takes the pieces; tosses them on the fire.)*

Gladys:
"And God called the light Day and the darkness he
called Night."
Sabina:
Pass up your chairs, everybody.
    (Voices in background rise in volume)
Save the human race.

FAST CURTAIN

ACT TWO

*Cabana in the Right end of orchestra pit is set up from
within it. MUSIC, "By the Sea." Two* Conveeners *enter from Cabana to set up ramp rails and
boardwalk, standards and rope rail. Music continues through this and finishes with the exit up
the auditorium aisle of the two* Conveeners.
*HOUSE LIGHTS OUT. ACT CURTAIN UP.
SOUND CUE #1. LIGHT CUE #1. Lantern
slide projections begin to appear on the curtain.
Time tables for trains leaving Pennsylvania sta-
tion for Atlantic City hotels, drugstores, churches,
rug merchants, fortune tellers, bingo parlors.*

The voice of an Announcer *is heard.*

Announcer:
(#1 slide)
The management now brings you the news events of
the world. Atlantic City, New Jersey:
(#15 slide)
This great convention city is playing host this week to
the anniversary convocation of that great fraternal
order
(#16 slide)
—the Ancient and Honorable Order of Mammals,
Subdivision Humans.
(#17 slide)
This great fraternal, militant and burial society is celebrating on the Boardwalk,
(#18 slide)
ladies and gentlemen, its six hundred thousandth An-
nual Convention. It has just elected its president
(#19 slide)
for the ensuing term—

51

(Projection of MR. *and* MRS. ANTROBUS *posed as they will be shown a few moments later)*

Mr. George Antrobus of Excelsior, New Jersey. We show you President Antrobus and his gracious and charming wife, every inch a mammal. Mr. Antrobus has had a long and checkered career. Credit has been paid to him for many useful enterprises including the introduction of the lever, of the wheel and the brewing of beer. Credit has also been extended to President Antrobus's gracious and charming wife for many practical suggestions, including the hem, the gore, and the gusset; and the novelty of the year,—frying in oil. Before we show you Mr. Antrobus accepting the nomination, we have an important announcement to make. As many of you know, this great celebration of the Order of the Mammals has received delegations from the other rival orders,—or shall we say: esteemed concurrent orders: the *Wings,* the *Fins,* the *Shells,* and so on. These orders are holding their conventions also, in various parts of the world, and have sent representatives to our own, two of a kind.

(Blackout projection)

Later in the day we will show you President Antrobus
(Traveller on screen open)
broadcasting his words of greeting and congratulation to the collected assemblies of the whole natural world.
(LIGHT CUE #2)
Ladies and Gentlemen! We give you President Antrobus!
(SOUND CUE #2)

(The screen becomes a transparency. ANTROBUS *and* MRS. ANTROBUS *are seated on bench Center. She is wearing a corsage of orchids.* ANTROBUS *wears an untidy Prince Albert; spats; from a red rosette in his buttonhole hangs a fine long purple ribbon of honor. He wears a gay lodge hat,— something between a fez and a legionnaire's cap.)*

ANTROBUS:
(Rises and quiets applause)
Fellow-mammals, fellow-vertebrates, fellow-humans, I

thank you. Little did my parents think,—when they told me to stand on my own two feet,—that I'd arrive at this place.

My friends, we have come a long way.

During this week of happy celebration it is perhaps not fitting that we dwell on some of the difficult times we have been through. The dinosaur is extinct—

(SOUND CUE #3)

—the ice has retreated; and the common cold is being pursued by every means within our power.

(MRS. ANTROBUS *sneezes, laughs prettily, and murmurs: "I beg your pardon."*)

In our memorial service yesterday we did honor to all our friends and relatives who are no longer with us, by reason of cold, earthquakes, plagues and—and—

(Coughs)

differences of opinion.

As our Bishop so ably said—uh—so ably said—

MRS. ANTROBUS:

Gone, but not forgotten.

ANTROBUS:

"They are gone, but not forgotten."

I think I can say, I think I can prophecy with complete —uh—with complete—

MRS. ANTROBUS:

Confidence.

ANTROBUS:

Thank you, my dear,— With complete lack of confidence, that a new day of security is about to dawn.

The watchword of the closing year was: work. I give you the watchword for the future: Enjoy yourselves.

MRS. ANTROBUS:

George, sit down!

ANTROBUS:

(A look of annoyance—he takes off glasses)

Before I close, however, I wish to answer one of those unjust and malicious accusations that were brought against me during this last electoral campaign.

Ladies and gentlemen, the charge was made that at various points in my career I leaned toward joining some of the rival orders,—that's a lie.

As I told reporters of the *Atlantic City Herald,* I do not deny that a few months before my birth I hesitated between — uh — between pinfeathers and gill-breathing,—and so did many of us here,—but for the last million years I have been viviparous, hairy and diaphragmatic. *(SOUND CUE #4)*

(Applause. Cries of "Good old Antrobus," "The Prince Chap," "Georgie," etc.)

ANNOUNCER:
Thank you. Thank you very much, Mr. Antrobus.
Now I know that our visitors will wish to hear a word from that gracious and charming mammal, Mrs. Antrobus, wife and mother,—Mrs. Antrobus!
(SOUND CUE #5)
MRS. ANTROBUS:
(Rises, bows and says)
Dear friends, I don't really think I should say anything. After all, it was my husband who was elected and not I.
Perhaps, as President of the Women's Auxiliary Bed and Board Society,—I had some notes here, oh, yes, here they are!—I should give a short report from some of our committees that have been meeting in this beautiful city.
Perhaps it may interest you to know that it has at last been decided that the tomato is edible. Can you all hear me? The tomato *is* edible.
A delegate from across the sea reports that the thread woven by the silkworm gives a cloth—I have a sample of it here—can you see it? Smooth, elastic. I should say that it's rather attractive,—though personally I prefer less shiny surfaces. Should the windows of a sleeping apartment be open or shut? I know all mothers will follow our debates on this matter with close interest. I am sorry to say that the most expert authorities have not yet decided. It does seem to me that the night air would be bound to be unhealthy for our children, but there are many distinguished authorities on both sides. Well, I could go on talking forever,—as

54

Shakespeare says: a woman's work is seldom done; but I think I'd better join my husband in saying thank you, and sit down. Thank you.

(She sits down.)

ANNOUNCER:

Oh, Mrs. Antrobus!

MRS. ANTROBUS:

(Rises)

Yes?

ANNOUNCER:

We understand that you are about to celebrate a wedding anniversary. I know our listeners would like to extend their felicitations and hear a few words from you on that subject.

MRS. ANTROBUS:

I have been asked by this kind gentleman—yes, my friends, this spring Mr. Antrobus and I will be celebrating our five thousandth wedding anniversary.

I don't know if I speak for my husband, but I can say that, as for me, I regret every moment of it.

(Laughter of confusion)

I beg your pardon. What I *mean* to say is that I do not regret one moment of it. I hope none of you catch my cold.

We have two children. We've always had two children, though it hasn't always been the same two. But as I say, we have two fine children, and we're very grateful for that.

Yes, Mr. Antrobus and I have been married five thousand years. Each wedding anniversary reminds me of the times when there were no weddings. We had to crusade for marriage. Perhaps there are some women within the sound of my voice who remember that crusade and those struggles; we fought for it, didn't we? We chained ourselves to lampposts and we made disturbances in the Senate,—anyway, at last we women got the ring.

(She adjusts her girdle)

A few men helped us, but I must say that most men blocked our way at every step: they said we were unfeminine.

I only bring up these unpleasant memories, because I
see some signs of backsliding from that great victory.
Oh, my fellow mammals, keep hold of that.
My husband says that the watchword for the year is
Enjoy Yourselves. I think that's very open to misun-
derstanding. My watchword for the year is: Save the
Family. It's held together for over five thousand years:
Save it! Thank you. *(SOUND Cue #6)*

> *(As she sits she sees* MR. ANTROBUS *has fallen
> asleep. She nudges him. He awakens with a start
> —starts applauding.)*

(LIGHT CUE #3)

(Traveller closed.)

ANNOUNCER:
Thank you, Mrs. Antrobus. *(SOUND CUE #7)*
(The transparency disappears)
We had hoped to show you the Beauty Contest that
took place here today.
President Antrobus, an experienced judge of pretty
girls, gave the title of Miss Atlantic City, 1942, to Miss
Lily-Sabina Fairweather, charming hostess of our
Boardwalk Bingo Parlor. *(FLY CUE #1)*
Unfortunately, however, our time is up, and I must
take you to some views of the Convention City and
conveeners,—enjoying themselves. *(LIGHT Cue #5)*
(SOUND CUE #8)

> *(The Boardwalk. The audience is sitting in the
> ocean. A handrail of scarlet cord stretches across
> the front of the stage. A ramp—also with scarlet
> hand rail—descends to the Right corner of the or-
> chestra pit where a great scarlet beach cabana
> stands. There are steps at Left from stage to
> pit. Center stage is a beach facing the sea. Stage
> Right is a street-lamp.)*
> *(The only scenery is two cardboard cutouts six
> feet high, representing shops at the back of the
> stage. Reading from Left to Right they are:
> Salt Water Taffy; Fortune Teller; then the blank
> space; Bingo Parlor; Turkish Bath. They have*

*practical doors, that of the Fortune Teller's being
hung with bright gypsy curtains.)
(Left of Fortune Teller's tent is the weather signal; it is like the mast of a ship with cross bars.
From time to time colored lights come on to indi-
cate the storm and hurrciane warnings. A roller
chair, pushed on Left by a melancholy* NEGRO,
files by off Right. It is occupied by a sleeping
CONVEENER *loaded with boardwalk gifts.)*

(From the cabana we hear voices)

CONVEENER:
(Imitating MRS. ANTROBUS*)*
My watchword for the coming year is save the family.
*(He enters running up the ramp to the stage, fol-
lowed by a* GIRL *dressed as a drum major)*
It's held together for five thousand years. Save it!
Thank you!
(Another CONVEENER, *followed by a* GIRL *dressed
as a drum major, follow the first pair up to the
stage. Then they run across laughing and shouting
and exit up Right.)*
CONVEENERS:
Enjoy yourselves!
GIRLS:
Enjoy yourselves!

(As the FOUR *from the cabana reach the stage, a*
MAN *and* WOMAN *enter arm in arm from up Left,
cross and exit up Right, following the* FOUR. *At
the same time the boardwalk chair with a sleeping*
CONVEENER *is pushed from down Right across the
stage to the up Left exit. As the* COUPLE *from up
Left pass the Fortune Teller's tent, the* FORTUNE
TELLER *and a* MIDGET *with a monkey's head enter
from tent. As they reach the end of the bench, a
loud "Bingo" comes from the Bingo Parlor which
causes parlor flat to jump and shudder. The* MON-
KEY CONVEENER *laughs and hands the* FORTUNE
TELLER *several bills and exits up Left. From the*

Bingo Parlor Two Conveeners *rush out, their hands full of bills. They pause a moment, amazed at all the money, and exit up Right. The* Fortune Teller *sits on the Left arm of bench and puts her money in her stocking. As she moves to the bench the* Two Conveeners *who came from the cabana enter from up Right and cross to Left.)*

(From the Bingo Parlor comes the voice of the caller)

Bingo Caller:
B-Nine; B-Nine. O-Twenty-six; O-Twenty-six.
N-Four; N-Four. I-Twelve, etc.
Chorus:
(Back-stage)
Bingo!!!
(The front of the Bingo Parlor shudders, rises a few feet in the air and returns to the ground, trembling.)
Fortune Teller:
(Mechanically, to the unconscious backs of Two Conveeners, *pointing with her pipe)*
Bright's disease!
(They pause a second with pain, then continue off up Left)
Your partner's deceiving you in that Kansas City deal.
You'll have six grandchildren. Avoid high places.
(She shouts after another Conveener *who has come from down Right and is passing in front of her)*
Cirrhosis of the liver!

(He stops a second with pain, then exits up Left.)

Sabina:
(Appears at the door of the Bingo Parlor. She hugs about her a white coat that almost conceals her red bathing suit. She crosses to the Fortune Teller *back of bench)*
Ssssst! Esmeralda! Sssst!

FORTUNE TELLER:
Keck!
SABINA:
Has President Antrobus come along yet?
FORTUNE TELLER:
No, no, no. Get back there. Hide yourself.
SABINA:
I'm afraid I'll miss him. Oh, Esmeralda, if I fail in
this, I'll die; I know I'll die.
FORTUNE TELLER:
Keck!
SABINA:
President Antrobus!!! And I'll be his wife! If it's the
last thing I'll do, I'll be Mrs. George Antrobus.—
Esmeralda, tell me my future.
FORTUNE TELLER:
Keck!
SABINA:
All right, I'll tell *you* my future.
> *(Laughing dreamily and tracing it out with one
> finger on the palm of her hand)*
I've won the Beauty Contest in Atlantic City,—well,
I'll win the Beauty Contest of the whole world. I'll
take President Antrobus away from that wife of his.
Then I'll take every man away from his wife. I'll turn
the whole earth upside down. When all those husbands
just think about me they'll get dizzy. They'll faint in
the streets. They'll have to lean against lampposts.—
Esmeralda, who was Helen of Troy?

> *(The* TWO CONVEENERS *from cabana enter from
> up Left carrying bottles of liquor.)*

FORTUNE TELLER:
> *(Furiously)*
Shut your foolish mouth.
When Mr. Antrobus comes along you can see what
you can do.
Until then,—go away.

> *(SABINA laughs. As she returns to the door of her*

Bingo Parlor, TWO CONVEENERS *rush over and smother her with attentions: "Oh, Miss Lily, you know me. You've known me for years.")*

SABINA:
Go away, boys, go away.
(One of the CONVEENERS *whispers in her ears)*
SABINA:
I'm after bigger fry than you are.—Why, Mr. Simpson!! How *dare* you?!! You forget yourself. It does not impress me that you are the commissioner of sanitation from Scranton, Pennsylvania. *(Exits.)*

(The CONVEENERS *squeal with pleasure and stumble in after her. The* SLEEPING CONVEENER *in the wheel chair is pushed across from up Left to up Right exit.)*

FORTUNE TELLER:
(Rises, unfurls her voluminous skirts, gives a sharp wrench to her bodice and strolls towards the audience, swinging her hips like a young woman)
I tell the future. Keck. Nothing easier. Everybody's future is in their face. Nothing easier.
But who can tell your past,—eh? Nobody!
Your youth,—where did it go? It slipped away while you weren't looking. While you were asleep. While you were drunk? Puh! You're like our friends, Mr. and Mrs. Antrobus; you lie awake nights trying to know your past. What did it mean? What was it trying to say to you?
Think! Think!
(An empty wheelchair is pushed by a forlorn-looking CHAIR-PUSHER *from up Left to up Right)*
Split your heads. I can't tell the past, and neither can you. If anybody tries to tell you the past, take my word for it, they're charlatans. But I can tell the future.
(She suddenly barks at a passing CHAIR-PUSHER *who is just passing the Bingo Parlor)*
Apoplexy!
(The CHAIR-PUSHER *stops a second, passes his*

hand across his forehead, then continues off up
Right. She returns to the audience)

Nobody listens.—Keck! I see a face among you now—
I won't embarrass him by pointing him out, but, listen, it may be you: Next year the watchspring inside
you will crumple up. Death by regret,—Type Y. It's in
the corners of your mouth. You'll decide that you
should have lived for pleasure, but that you missed it.
Death by regret,—Type Y— Avoid mirrors. You'll
try to be angry,—but no!—no anger.

(Far forward, confidentially)

And now what's the immediate future of our friends,
the Antrobuses? Oh, you've seen it as well as I have,
keck,—that dizziness of the head; that Great Man
dizziness? The inventor of beer and gunpowder. The
sudden fits of temper and then the long stretches of
inertia? "I'm a sultan; let my slave-girls fan me"?
You know as well as I what's coming. Rain. Rain. Rain
in floods. The deluge. But first you'll see shameful
things—shameful things.

Shameful things. Some of you will be saying: "Let
him drown. He's not worth saving. Give the whole
thing up." I can see it in your faces. But you're wrong.
Keep your doubts and despairs to yourselves.

Again there'll be the narrow escape. The survival of a
handful. From destruction,—total destruction.

(The crowd of CONVEENERS and GIRLS enter: Two
MEN from Bingo; two MEN and two GIRLS from
down Right to lamppost; two MEN and one GIRL
form up Left to banner down Left; one MAN
from behind tent to weather signal. She points,
sweeping with her hand to the stage)

Even of the animals, a few will be saved: two of a
kind, male and female, two of a kind.

(The CONVEENERS appear about the stage, jeering
at her with animal sounds and raucous laughter.)

CONVEENERS:
    (MAN down Left)   *(MAN down Right)*
Charlatan!   Madam Kill-Joy!

　　　　(MAN *up Right*)　　　　　(MAN *up Left*)
Mrs. Jeremiah!　　　　　　Charlatan!
FORTUNE TELLER:
　　　　(*Turns on them sharply and crosses to the* TWO
　　　　at the Bingo Parlor)
And *you!* Mark my words before it's too late. Where'll
you be?

　　　　(*The group of* FOUR *down Right stick their
　　　　tongues out at her. She moves toward them.*)

CONVEENERS:
　　　　(MAN *off Right*)
The croaking raven.
　　　　(GIRL *down Right*)
Old dust and ashes.
　　　　(MEN *down Left*)
Rags, bottles, sacks.
FORTUNE TELLER:
Yes, stick out your tongues. You can't stick your
tongues out far enough to lick the death-sweat from
your foreheads. It's too late
　　　　(*SCREAMS and LAUGHTER come from off
　　　　Left. She crosses to* GROUP *Left Center*)
to work now—bail out the flood with your soup spoons.
You've had your chance and you've lost.
CONVEENERS:
Enjoy yourselves!!!!

　　　　(*They disappear. The* FORTUNE TELLER *looks off
　　　　Right and puts her finger on her lip.*)

FORTUNE TELLER.
They're coming, the Antrobuses. Keck. Your hope.
　　　　(*Crossing down Left to banner*)
Your despair. Your selves.

　　　　(*Enter from up Right* GLADYS *and* MR. *and* MRS.
　　　　ANTROBUS. GLADYS *crosses to down Left.* ANTRO-
　　　　BUS *to Right of* GLADYS. MRS. ANTROBUS *to above
　　　　bench.*)

MRS. ANTROBUS:
Gladys, Gladys Antrobus, stick your stummick in.
GLADYS:
But it's easier this way.
MRS. ANTROBUS:
(As ANTROBUS *takes a digestion pill from bottle)*
Well, it's too bad the new president has such a clumsy
daughter, that's all I can say. Try and be a lady.
FORTUNE TELLER:
Aijah! That's been said a hundred billion times.
MRS. ANTROBUS:
Goodness! Where's Henry? He was here a minute ago.
Henry!

> *(Sudden violent stir.* TWO CONVEENERS *run on
> quickly, followed by a roller-chair from up
> Right. About it are dancing in great excitement*
> HENRY *and a* NEGRO CHAIR-PUSHER. *As they reach
> Right Center the* CHAIR-PUSHER *pulls the chair
> from* HENRY *and rights it.* HENRY *looks to the*
> CONVEENERS *at his Left for encouragement. They
> urge him on.)*

HENRY:
> *(Slingshot in hand, advancing on the* CHAIR-
> PUSHER*)*
I'll put your eye out. I'll make you yell, like you never
yelled before.
NEGRO:
> *(At the same time)*
Now, I warns you. I warns you. If you make me mad,
you'll get hurt.
ANTROBUS:
Henry! What is this? Put down that slingshot.
MRS. ANTROBUS:
> *(At the same time. Crossing to* HENRY *to straight-
> en his hair and tie)*
Henry! *Henry!* Behave yourself.
FORTUNE TELLER:
> *(Crossing front of* ANTROBUS *to tent)*
That's right, young man. There are too many people

in the world as it is. Everybody's in the way, except one's self.

> *(Exits into her tent.)*

HENRY:

All I wanted to do was—have some fun.

NEGRO:

Fun? You get clean away from me and you get away fast. Nobody can't touch my chair, nobody, without I allow 'em to.

> *(He pushes his chair off up Left, muttering, followed by the two* CONVEENERS.*)*

ANTROBUS:

What were you doing, Henry?

HENRY:

> *(Crossing down Left)*

Everybody's always getting mad. Everybody's always trying to push you around. I'll make him sorry for this; I'll make him sorry.

ANTROBUS:

> *(Crossing to above bench)*

Give me that slingshot.

> *(*GLADYS *crosses to bench; sits.)*

HENRY:

I won't. I'm sorry I came to this place. I wish I weren't here.

> *(Crosses to lamppost, facing away)*

I wish I weren't anywhere.

MRS. ANTROBUS:

Now, Henry, don't get so excited about nothing. I declare I don't know what we're going to do with you. Put your slingshot in your pocket and don't try to take hold of things that don't belong to you.

ANTROBUS:

After this you can stay home. I wash my hands of you.

MRS. ANTROBUS:

> *(Crosses to* ANTROBUS, *pushes his pocket handkerchief down into the pocket. Annoyed, he pulls it out)*

Come now, let's forget all about it.

> *(*BOTH *cross Left)*

Everybody
  (CONVEENER *enters from up Left to down Center*)
take a good breath of that sea air and calm down.
  (*The passing* CONVEENER *bows to* ANTROBUS, *who
  nods to him*)
Who was that you spoke to, George?
ANTROBUS:
Nobody, Maggie. Just the candidate who ran against
me in the election.
MRS. ANTROBUS:
The man who ran against you in the election!!
  (*She turns, crosses up Right and waves her um-
  brella after the disappearing* CONVEENER, *whom
  she has caught laughing at them*)
My husband didn't speak to you and he never will
speak to you.
ANTROBUS:
Now, Maggie.
MRS. ANTROBUS:
  (*Calling off up Right*)
After those lies you told about him in your speeches!
Lies, that's what they were.

  (ANTROBUS *to bench; sits Left end.*)

GLADYS:
Mama, everybody's looking at you.
HENRY:
Everybody's laughing at you.
MRS. ANTROBUS:
If you must know, my husband's a *saint*, a downright
saint, and you're not fit to speak to him on the street.
ANTROBUS:
Now, Maggie, now Maggie, that's enough of that.
MRS. ANTROBUS:
George Antrobus, you're a perfect worm. If you won't
stand up for yourself, I will.
GLADYS:
Mama, you just act awful in public.
MRS. ANTROBUS:
  (*Laughing*)

Well, I must say I enjoyed it. I feel better. Wish his wife had been there to hear it.

(Crosses to bench; sits Right end.)

(The Two Men *and* Two Girls *who came from the cabana are pushed across in a roller chair by the* Negro *who fought with* Henry—*from up Left to up Right. The* Girls *and* Men *are embracing)*

Children, what do you want to do?

GLADYS:

Mama, can we ride in one of those chairs? Mama, Papa, I want to ride in one of those chairs.

(Henry *crosses to Right end bench, watching the chair roll by.)*

MRS. ANTROBUS:

No, sir. If you're tired you just sit where you are. We have no money to spend on foolishness.

ANTROBUS:

I guess we have money enough for a thing like that. It's one of the things you do at Atlantic City.

(Takes coin purse from pocket.)

MRS. ANTROBUS:

Oh, we have?

(Pulls GLADYS' *dress down to cover knees)*

I tell you it's a miracle my children have shoes to stand up in. I didn't think I'd ever live to see them pushed around in chairs.

(Henry *crosses up to Turkish Bath door.)*

ANTROBUS:

(Takes out roll of bills)

We're on a vacation, aren't we? We have a right to some treats, I guess. Maggie, some day you're going to drive me crazy.

(Hands a bill to GLADYS.*)*

MRS. ANTROBUS:

All right, go. I'll just sit here and laugh at you. And you can give me my dollar right in my hand. Mark my

words, a rainy day is coming. There's a rainy day
ahead of us. I feel it in my bones.
(He hands her a bill)
Go on throw your money around. I can starve. I've
starved before. I know how.
CONVEENER:
*(Puts his head out of Turkish Bath window and
says with raised eyebrows)*
Hello, George. How are ya? I see where you brought
the *whole* family along.
MRS. ANTROBUS:
And what do you mean by that?

(CONVEENER *withdraws and closes window.*)

ANTROBUS:
(Rises)
Maggie, I tell you there's a limit to what I can stand.
God's Heaven, haven't I worked *enough?* Don't I get
any vacation? Can't I even give my children so much
as a ride in a roller-chair?
(Crosses to Right of bench—above it.)
MRS. ANTROBUS:
(Putting out her hand for raindrops)
Anyway, it's going to rain very soon and you have
your broadcast to make.
ANTROBUS:
(Turns to her)
Now, Maggie, I warn you.
(Steps up stage)
You're driving me crazy.
(Turns to her)
A man can stand a family only just so long. I'm warn-
ing you.
(He steps up to Right of Bingo.)

*(Enter SABINA from the Bingo Parlor. She wears
a flounced red silk bathing suit, 1905. Red stock-
ings, shoes, parasol. She bows demurely to AN-
TROBUS, crosses Left and starts down the ramp.
ANTROBUS and the CHILDREN stare at her. AN-
TROBUS bows gallantly and follows her across stage.*

Henry starts to follow them, then quickly moves down Right to rail to watch her descend the ramp to cabana.)

MRS. ANTROBUS:
Why, George Antrobus, how can you say such a thing? You have the best family in the world.

ANTROBUS:
Good morning, Miss Fairweather.
    (Sabina finally disappears into the cabana.)

MRS. ANTROBUS:
Who on earth was that you spoke to, George?

ANTROBUS:
    (Complacent; mock-modest)
Hm—m—just a—solambaka keray.

MRS. ANTROBUS:
What? I can't understand you.

GLADYS:
Mama, wasn't she beautiful?

HENRY:
Papa, introduce her to me.

MRS. ANTROBUS:
Children, will you be quiet while I ask your father a simple question?—Who did you say it was, George?

ANTROBUS:
Why—uh—a friend of mine. Very nice refined girl.

MRS. ANTROBUS:
I'm waiting.

ANTROBUS:
    (Crossing to bench)
Maggie, that's the girl I gave the prize to in the beauty contest,—that Miss Atlantic City 1942.
    (Steps up Left.)

MRS. ANTROBUS:
Hm! She looked like Sabina to me.

HENRY:
    (At the railing down Right)
Mama, the lifeguard knows her, too. Mama, he knows her well.

ANTROBUS:
Henry, come here.

(Crosses to bench. HENRY *moves away from rail,
circles and comes down to it again)*
—She's a very nice girl in every way and the sole support of her aged mother.
(Step up Left.)
MRS. ANTROBUS:
So was Sabina, so was Sabina; and it took a wall of
ice to open your eyes about Sabina.—Henry, come over
and sit down on this bench.

(HENRY *steps away, then goes back to rail.)*

ANTROBUS:
(Crossing down to bench)
She's a very different matter from Sabina. Miss Fairweather is a college graduate, Phi Beta Kappa.
MRS. ANTROBUS:
Henry, you sit here by Mama.
(Pulls down GLADYS' *dress)*
Gladys—

(HENRY *crosses to bench. Sits on Right arm, facing up.)*

ANTROBUS:
Reduced circumstances have required her taking a
position as hostess in a Bingo Parlor; but there isn't a
girl with higher principles in the country.
(Step away.)
MRS. ANTROBUS:
Well, let's not talk about it.—Henry, I haven't seen a
whale yet.
ANTROBUS:
(Crossing to her)
She speaks seven languages and has more culture in
her little finger than you've acquired in a lifetime.
(Crosses down Left. Looks to cabana.)

(HENRY *spots the weather signals—rises, moves
toward it, slingshot in hand—takes aim.)*

MRS. ANTROBUS:
(Assumed amiability)
All right, all right, George. I'm glad to know there are such superior girls in the Bingo Parlors.
(Looks around)
—Henry, what's that?
(Pointing at the weather signal, which has one light on.)

(ANTROBUS to bench—sits Left end.)

HENRY:
(Crossing up Left)
What is it, Papa?
ANTROBUS:
What? Oh, that's the storm signal. One of those lights means bad weather; two means storm; three means hurricane; and four means the end of the world.
(LIGHT CUE #6)

(As they watch it a second light snaps on.)

MRS. ANTROBUS:
Goodness! I'm going this very minute to buy you all some raincoats.
GLADYS:
(Putting her cheek against her father's shoulder)
Mama, don't go yet. I like sitting this way. And the ocean coming in and coming in. Papa, don't you like it?
ANTROBUS:
H-m-m-m!
MRS. ANTROBUS:
Well, there's only one thing I lack to make me a perfectly happy woman: I'd like to see a whale.
HENRY:
Mama, we saw two. Right out there. They're delegates to the convention.
(Crossing down Left to platform, looking front.)
GLADYS:
Papa, ask me something. Ask me a question.
ANTROBUS:
Well—how big's the ocean?

70

GLADYS:
Papa, you're teasing me. It's—three hundred and sixty
million square miles—-and—it—covers—three-fourths
—of—the—earth's—surface—and—its—deepest place
—is—five—and—a—half—miles—deep—and — its —
average—depth — is — twelve — thousand — feet. No,
Papa, ask me something hard, real hard.
MRS. ANTROBUS:
    (Rising)
Now I'm going off to buy those raincoats. I think that
bad weather's going to get worse and worse. I hope it
doesn't come before your broadcast. I should think we
have about an hour or so.
HENRY:
I hope it comes and
    (Airplane gesture)
everything before it. I hope it—
    (Machine gun sound and buzz.)
MRS. ANTROBUS:
Henry!
    (HENRY *aims at her with louder gun sounds)*
Henry!
    (HENRY *crosses up Left)*
—George, I think
    (Crossing to Left of ANTROBUS*)*
—maybe, it's one of those storms that are just as bad
on land as on the sea. When you're just as safe and
safer in a good stout boat.
HENRY:
    (Turns to them)
There's a boat out at the end of the pier.
MRS. ANTROBUS:
Well, keep your eye on it.
    (Pushes his handkerchief in pocket)
George, you shut your eyes and get a good rest before
the broadcast.
ANTROBUS:
Thundering Judas, do I have to be told when to open
and shut my eyes?
    (He pulls out the handkerchief)
Go and buy your raincoats.

MRS. ANTROBUS:
Now, children, you have ten minutes to walk around.
Ten minutes.
>   (HENRY *starts running. She catches him as he*
>   *passes*)
And Henry: control yourself.
>   (HENRY *exits up Right*)
Gladys, stick by your brother and don't get lost.
>   (GLADYS *kisses* ANTROBUS *and exits after* HENRY.)
>   (TWO CONVEENERS, *arm in arm, enter up Left,*
>   *strolling*)
>   (MRS. ANTROBUS, *crossing to him above bench*)
Will you be all right, George?

>   (CONVEENERS *start talking as they are crossing.*)

1ST CONVEENER:
George.
2ND CONVEENER:
Geo-r-r-rge!
1ST CONVEENER:
Georgiee!
2ND CONVEENER:
Leave the old hencoop at home.
1ST CONVEENER:
George. Do-mes-ticated Georgie!
>   *(They exit up Right.)*
MRS. ANTROBUS:
>   *(Shaking her umbrella)*
Low common oafs!
>   (FORTUNE TELLER *enters from tent to down Left,*
>   *watching cabana*)
That's what they are.
>   *(Crossing to Left end bench)*
Guess a man has a right to bring his wife to a con-
vention, if he wants to. What's the matter with a fam-
>   *(She pushes the handkerchief down)*
ily, I'd like to know.
>   (SABINA *enters from cabana*)
Hm'p—what else have they got to offer?
>   *(Crosses Right.)*

(Exits up Right. ANTROBUS has closed his eyes. The FORTUNE TELLER is watching SABINA quizzically.)

FORTUNE TELLER:
Heh! Here she comes!

SABINA:
(Loud whisper as she comes up the ramp)
What's he doing?

FORTUNE TELLER:
Oh, he's ready for you. Bite your lips, dear, take a long breath and come on up.

SABINA:
(At Left of FORTUNE TELLER)
I'm nervous. My whole future depends on this. I'm nervous.

FORTUNE TELLER:
Don't be a fool. What more could you want? He's forty-five. His head's a little dizzy. He's just been elected president. He's never known any other woman than his wife. Whenever he looks at her he realizes that she knows every foolish thing he's ever done.

SABINA:
(Crosses Right, then turns back to FORTUNE TELLER, still whispering)
I don't know why it is, but every time I start one of these I'm nervous.
(The FORTUNE TELLER laughs drily and makes the gesture of impatience; steps up Left; faces off. SABINA goes to Left end bench, coughs and says:)
Oh, Mr. Antrobus,—dare I speak to you for a moment?

ANTROBUS:
(Looks around, rises quickly, backs away Right, pulls out handkerchief and straightens coat)
What?—Oh, certainly, certainly, Miss Fairweather.

SABINA:
(Crossing to front of bench)
Mr. Antrobus—I've been so unhappy. I've wanted— I've wanted to make sure that you don't think that I'm the kind of girl who goes out for beauty contests.

FORTUNE TELLER:
That's the way!
ANTROBUS:
Oh, I understand. I understand perfectly.
FORTUNE TELLER:
Give it a little more. Lean on it.
SABINA:
I knew you would. My mother said to me this morn-
ing: Lily, she said, that fine Mr. Antrobus gave you
the prize because he saw at once that you weren't the
kind of girl who'd go in for a thing like that.
(Sits bench)
But, honestly, Mr. Antrobus, in this world, honestly, a
good girl doesn't know where to turn.
FORTUNE TELLER:
Now you've gone too far.
ANTROBUS:
My dear Miss Fairweather!
SABINA:
You wouldn't know how hard it is. With that lovely
wife and daughter you have. Oh, I think Mrs. An-
trobus is the finest woman I ever saw. I wish I were
like her.
ANTROBUS:
There, there.
(Sits bench to her Right)
There's—room for all kinds of people in the world,
Miss Fairweather. *(He laughs.)*
SABINA:
(She joins his laughter)
How wonderful of you to say that. How generous!—
Mr. Antrobus, have you a moment free?—I'm afraid
I may be a little conspicuous here—could you come
down, for just a moment, to my beach cabana—
ANTROBUS:
Why—uh—yes, certainly—for a moment
(Quick glance off Right)
—just for a moment.
SABINA:
There's a nice, comfortable deck chair there. Because:
you know you *do* look tired. Just this morning my

74   ACT II

mother said to me: Lily, she said, I hope Mr. Antrobus is getting a good rest. His fine strong face has deep lines in it. Now isn't it true, Mr. Antrobus: you work too hard?

FORTUNE TELLER:

Bingo! *(She exits into tent.)*

(They BOTH rise. SABINA takes his hand and pulls him gently to the platform leading to ramp down Left.)

SABINA:

Now you come along and just stretch out in my cabana. No, I shan't say a word, not a word.

I shall just sit there,—privileged.

(She stops halfway down ramp)

That's what I am.

ANTROBUS:

(Taking her arms for an embrace)

Miss Fairweather—you'll—spoil me.

SABINA:

(Stopping the embrace)

Just a moment. I have something I wish to say to the audience.—Ladies and gentlemen. I'm not going to play this particular scene tonight. It's just a short scene and we're going to skip it. But I'll tell you what takes place and then we can continue the play from there on. Now in this scene—

ANTROBUS:

(Between his teeth)

But, Miss Somerset!

SABINA:

I'm sorry. I'm sorry. But I have to skip it.

(ANTROBUS crosses to up Left, looking off)

In this scene, I talk to Mr. Antrobus, and at the end of it he decides to leave his wife, get a divorce at Reno and marry me. That's all.

ANTROBUS:

(Calling)

Fitz!

SABINA:

So that now I've told you we can jump to the end of it.

(ANTROBUS *to Right Center above bench*)
Where you say:
(Turns)
Where is he?
(Enter from up Right in fury FITZPATRICK, *the stage manager. He crosses down Center.)*
FITZPATRICK:
Miss Somerset, we insist on your playing this scene.

(A CONVEENER *enters from down Right; crosses to* ANTROBUS. *A* CHAIR-PUSHER *enters from up Center; crosses to* ANTROBUS.)*

SABINA:
I'm sorry, Mr. Fitzpatrick, but I can't and I won't.
*(FORTUNE TELLER *enters from tent; crosses to back of bench)*
I've told the audience all they need know and now we can go on.
(Other ACTORS *begin to appear on the stage, listening.)*
FITZPATRICK:
And *why* can't you play it?

(TWO CONVEENERS *and* TWO GIRLS *who rode across in roller chair enter from up Left—stand together down Left.)*

SABINA:
Because there are some lines in that scene that would hurt some people's feelings and I don't think the theatre is a place where people's feelings ought to be hurt.
(TWO CONVEENERS *enter from down Right; stand out Right proscenium.)*
FITZPATRICK:
Miss Somerset, you can pack up your things and go home. I shall call the understudy and I shall report you to Equity.
SABINA:
I sent the understudy up to the corner for a cup of

ACT II

coffee and if Equity tries to penalize me I'll drag the case right up to the Supreme Court.

FITZPATRICK:

Why can't you play it—

ANTROBUS:

(Crossing down Center)

What's the matter with the scene?

SABINA:

Well, if you must know, I have a personal guest in the audience tonight. Her life hasn't been exactly a happy one. I wouldn't have my friend hear some of these lines for the whole world.

(ANTROBUS sits bench)

I don't suppose it occurred to the author that some other women might have gone through the experience of losing their husbands like this. Wild horses wouldn't drag from me the details of my friend's life, but— well, they'd been married twenty years, and before he got rich, why, she'd done the washing and everything. As for the other harrowing details, well—

(WOMAN in audience bursts into loud sobbing, which attracts the attention of all on stage.)

FITZPATRICK:

(As SABINA looks up at him)

Miss Somerset, your friend will forgive you. We must play this scene.

SABINA:

Nothing, nothing will make me say some of those lines —about "a man outgrows a wife every seven years" and—and that one about "the Mohammedans being the only people who looked the subject square in the face."

FITZPATRICK:

(Step back)

Miss Somerset! Go to your dressing room. I'll *read* your lines myself!

(FORTUNE TELLER exits to tent.)

SABINA:

Now everybody's nerves are on edge.

ANTROBUS:
Skip the scene!
(Puts out cigarette; crosses to ramp.)
SABINA:
(To the ACTORS*)*
Thank you. I knew you'd understand.
(Other CONVEENERS *repeat "Skip it" and exit.*
FITZPATRICK *exits up Right)*
(To audience)
We'll do just what I said.
So Mr. Antrobus is going to divorce his wife and
marry me. Mr. Antrobus, you say: "It won't be easy
to lay all this before my wife."
(The ACTORS *withdraw.)*
ANTROBUS:
*(Crosses to her Right on ramp, his hand to his
forehead, muttering)*
Wait a minute. I can't get back into it as easily as all
that. "My wife is a very obstinate woman." Hm—then
you say —hm— Miss Fairweather, I mean Lily, it
won't be easy to lay all this before my wife. It'll hurt
her feelings a little.
SABINA:
Listen, George: *other* people haven't got feelings. Not
in the same way that we have,—we who are presidents
like you and prize-winners like me. Listen, other
people haven't got feelings; they just imagine they
have. Within two weeks they go back to playing bridge
and going to the movies.
Listen, dear: everybody in the world except a few
people like you and me are just people of straw. Most
people have no insides at all. Now that you're president
you'll see that. Listen, darling, there's a kind of secret
society at the top of the world,—like you and me,—that
know this. The world was made for us. What's life
anyway? Except for two things, pleasure and power,
what is life? Boredom! Foolishness! You know it is.
Except for those two things, life's nau-se-ating. So,—
come here!
(They embrace—long kiss. SABINA *crossing down*
78   ACT II

ramp to cabana ahead of him—he follows, dazed)
Now when your wife comes, it's really very simple.
(She turns to him)
Just tell her.
ANTROBUS:
Lily, Lily: you're a wonderful woman.
SABINA:
Of course I am. *(SOUND CUE #9)*
(LIGHT CUE #7)

*(ANTROBUS enters cabana followed by SABINA.
Distant roll of THUNDER. A third LIGHT appears on the weather signal. The large roller chair
with the CHAIR-PUSHER seated and being pushed
by the TWO CONVEENERS who were seen riding in
it, being driven by the TWO GIRLS enter from up
Left, tour and exit up Right. MRS. ANTROBUS appears carrying a raincoat from up Right. She looks
about, seats herself on the bench and fans herself
with her handkerchief. Enter GLADYS down Right.
She bounds toward her mother. She is wearing red
stockings. She is followed by TWO CONVEENERS.
They whistle at her as they are crossing from
Right to Left. As they reach up Left MRS. AN-
TROBUS looks around, sees GLADYS and calls her.)*

GLADYS:
(Crossing to bench—sits)
Mama, here I am.

*(The TWO CONVEENERS watch this, look at each
other, whistle, and exit up Left.)*

MRS. ANTROBUS:
Gladys Antrobus!!! Where did you get those dreadful
things?
GLADYS:
Wha-a-t? Papa liked the color.
MRS. ANTROBUS:
You go back to the hotel this minute!
GLADYS:
(Rises—steps away)

I won't. I won't. Papa liked the color.

MRS. ANTROBUS:

All right. All right. You stay here. I've a good mind to let your father see you that way. You stay right here.

GLADYS:

I—I don't want to stay if—if you don't think he'd like it.

MRS. ANTROBUS:

Oh—it's all one to me. I don't care what happens. I don't care if the biggest storm in the whole world comes. Let it come.

(She folds her hands)

Where's your brother?

GLADYS:

(In a small voice)

He'll be here.

MRS. ANTROBUS:

Will he? Well, let him get into trouble. I don't care. I don't know where your father is, I'm sure.

(A burst of laughter comes from the cabana and the cabana shudders with excitement.)

GLADYS:

(Leaning over the rail)

I think he's— Mama, he's talking to the lady in the red dress.

MRS. ANTROBUS:

Is that so?

(Pause)

We'll wait till he's through. Sit down here beside me

(GLADYS *sits bench*) *(SOUND CUE #10)*

—and stop fidgeting.

(GLADYS *rests her head on* MRS. ANTROBUS' *shoulder)*

What are you crying about?

(BROADCAST OFFICIAL and ASSISTANT rush in with a microphone on a standard.)

GLADYS:

You don't like my stockings.

BROADCAST OFFICIAL:
> *(Crossing to Right of bench.* ASSISTANT *places mike Right Center and sets it up)*

Mrs. Antrobus. Thank God we've found you at last. Where's Mr. Antrobus? We've been hunting everywhere for him. It's about time for the broadcast to the conventions of the world.

MRS. ANTROBUS:
> *(Calm—covering* GLADYS' *legs with raincoat, tucking it around)*

I expect he'll be here in a minute.

> (ASSISTANT *crosses up Left above bench.)*

BROADCAST OFFICIAL:
Mrs. Antrobus, if he doesn't show up in time, I hope you will consent to broadcast in his place. It's the most important broadcast of the year.

> (SABINA *enters from cabana, wearing white coat, dark glasses, and smoking cigarette.)*

MRS. ANTROBUS:
No, I shan't. I haven't one single thing to say.

> (ASSISTANT *down front to platform.)*

BROADCAST OFFICIAL:
Then won't you help us find him, Mrs. Antrobus, a storm's coming up. A hurricane. A deluge!

ASSISTANT:
> *(Who has sighted* ANTROBUS *over the rail)*

Miss Fairweather, have you seen—
> (ANTROBUS *enters from cabana)*

Joe! Joe! Here he is. *(Exits up Left.)*

BROADCAST OFFICIAL:
> *(Crossing above bench to platform, talking to* ANTROBUS, *who is coming up ramp, followed by* SABINA)*

In the name of God, Mr. Antrobus, you're on the air in five minutes. Will you kindly please come and test

the instrument? That's all we ask. If you just please
begin the alphabet slowly.

(ANTROBUS, *with set face, comes ponderously up
the ramp. He stops on the platform. Authorita-
tively to the* OFFICIAL)   *(SOUND CUE #11)*

ANTROBUS:
I'll be ready when the time comes. Until then, move
away. Go away!
    (BROADCAST OFFICIAL *steps aside Left.* ANTRO-
    BUS *goes to Left of bench)*
I have something I wish to say to my wife.
BROADCAST OFFICIAL:
    (Whimpering)
Mr. Antrobus! This is the most important broadcast
of the year.
    (The OFFICIAL *withdraws to the edge of the stage.)*
                              (LIGHT CUE #7A)
SABINA:
    (Behind ANTROBUS. *Whispering)*
Don't let her argue. Remember arguments have noth-
ing to do with it.

    (BROADCAST OFFICIAL *crosses up Center; takes
    off his fez.)*

ANTROBUS:
Maggie, I'm moving out of the hotel. In fact, I'm moving out of everything. For good. I'm going to marry
Miss Fairweather. I shall provide generously for you
and the children. In a few years you'll be able to see
that it's all for the best. That's all I have to say:

BROADCAST OFFICIAL:	BINGO ANNOUNCER:
Mr. Antrobus! I h o p e	B—nine; B—nine.
you'll be ready. This is the	N—forty-two; N—forty-
most important broadcast	two;
of the year.	O—thirty; O—thirty.
GLADYS:	B—seventeen; B—seven-
What did P a p a say,	teen.
Mama? I didn't hear what	I—forty; I—forty.
he said.	

BROADCAST OFFICIAL:
 (Crosses to Right of
  ANTROBUS)
Mr. Antrobus. A l l w e
want to do is test your
voice with the alphabet.
ANTROBUS:
Go away. Clear out.

CHORUS:
Bingo!!

 (BROADCAST OFFICIAL *backs away up Center.*)
MRS. ANTROBUS: *(SOUND CUE #12)*
 (Composedly with lowered eyes)
George, I can't talk to you until you wipe those silly
red marks off your face.
ANTROBUS:
I think there's nothing to talk about. I've said what I
have to say.
SABINA:
Splendid!!
ANTROBUS:
You're a fine woman, Maggie, but—but a man has his
own life to lead in the world.
MRS. ANTROBUS:
Well, after living with you for five thousand years I
guess I have a right to a word or two, haven't I?
ANTROBUS:
 (To SABINA)
What can I answer to that?
SABINA:
Tell her that conversation would only hurt her feelings.
It's-kinder-in-the-long-run-to-do-it-short-and-quick.
ANTROBUS:
I want to spare your feelings in every way I can,
Maggie.
BROADCAST OFFICIAL:
 (Crossing Right to mike—indicates weather signal)
Mr. Antrobus, the hurricane signal's gone up. We
could begin right now.
MRS. ANTROBUS:
 (Calmly, almost dreamily)
I didn't marry you because you were perfect, George.

I didn't even marry you because I loved you. I married
you because you gave me a promise.
That promise made up for your faults. And the promise I gave you made up for mine. Two imperfect people
got married and it was the promise that made the
marriage.

ANTROBUS:

Maggie, I was only nineteen.

MRS. ANTROBUS:

And when our children were growing up, it wasn't a
house that protected them; and it wasn't our love that
protected them—it was that promise.

And when that promise is broken—this can happen.

*(With a sweep of the hand she removes the rain-
coat from GLADYS' stockings and rises.)*

(BROADCAST OFFICIAL steps down, watching.)
(LIGHT CUE #7B)

ANTROBUS:

(Stretches out his arm, apoplectic)

Gladys!! Have you gone crazy? Has everyone gone
crazy?

(Turning on SABINA)

You did this. You gave them to her.

SABINA:

I never said a word to her.

ANTROBUS:

(To GLADYS)

You go back to the hotel and take those horrible things
off.

GLADYS:

(Pert)

Before I go, I've got something to tell you,—it's about
Henry.

MRS. ANTROBUS:

Stop your

(Hand on GLADYS' shoulder)

noise,—I'm taking her back

(Crossing to Left end of bench)

to the hotel, George. Before I go I have a letter—I
have a message to throw into the ocean.

(Fumbling in her handbag)
Where is the plagued thing? Here it is.
(She flings something—invisible to us—far over the heads of the audience to the back of the auditorium)
It's a botttle. And in the bottle's a letter. And in the letter is written all the things that a woman knows.
It's never been told to any man and it's never been told to any woman, and if it finds its destination, a new time will come. We're not what books and plays say we are. We're not what advertisements say we are. We're not in the movies and we're not on the radio.
We're not what you're all told and what you think we are: We're ourselves. And if any man can find one of us he'll learn why the whole universe was set in motion. And if any man harm any of us, his soul—the only soul he's got—had better be at the bottom of that ocean, —and that's the only way to put it. Gladys, come here. We're going back to the hotel. *(LIGHT CUE #8)*
(She drags GLADYS *firmly off Left by the hand, front of* ANTROBUS *and* SABINA.*)*
SABINA:
Such goings-on.
(Step to ANTROBUS*)*
Don't give it a minute's thought.
GLADYS:
(Enters from up Left; crosses to them)
Anyway, I think you ought to know that Henry hit a man with a stone. He hit one of those colored men that push the chairs and the man's very sick. Henry ran away and hid and some policemen are looking for him very hard. And I don't care a bit if you don't want to have anything to do with Mama and me, because I'll never like you again and I hope nobody ever likes you again,—so there! *(She runs off up Left.)*
ANTROBUS:
(Starts to go)
I—I have to go and see what I can do about this.
SABINA:
(Stopping him)
You stay right here. Don't you go now while you're

excited. Gracious sakes, all these things will be forgotten in a hundred years.

(Walking Right to mike)

Come, now, you're on the air.

BROADCAST OFFICIAL:

Thank you, Miss Fairweather.

SABINA:

Just say anything,—it doesn't matter what. Just a lot of birds and fishes and things.

BROADCAST OFFICIAL:

Thank you, Miss Fairweather. Thank you very much. Ready, Mr. Antrobus.   *(SOUND CUE #13)*

ANTROBUS:

(Touching the mike, BROADCAST OFFICIAL to his Right. SABINA to his Left)

What is it? What is it? Who am I talking to?

BROADCAST OFFICIAL:

Why, Mr. Antrobus! To our order and to all the other orders.

ANTROBUS:

(Raising his head)

What are all those birds doing?

BROADCAST OFFICIAL:

Those are just a few of the birds. Those are the delegates to our convention,—two of a kind.

ANTROBUS:

(Pointing into the audience)

Look at the water. Look at them all. Those fishes jumping. The children should see this!—There's Maggie's whales!!

(Turning to SABINA)

Here are your whales, Maggie.

BROADCAST OFFICIAL:

I hope you're ready, Mr. Antrobus.

ANTROBUS:

And look on the beach! You didn't tell me these would be here!

SABINA:

Yes, George. Those are the animals.

BROADCAST OFFICIAL: *(SOUND CUE #13A)*

Yes, Mr. Antrobus, those are the vertebrates. We hope

86   ACT II

the lion will have a word to say when you're through. Step right up, Mr. Antrobus, we're ready. We'll just have time before the storm.

(Pause. In a hoarse whisper)

They're waiting. *(PROPERTY CUE #1)*

(It has grown dark. Soon after he speaks a high whistling NOISE begins.)

ANTROBUS:

Friends. Cousins. Fourscore and ten million years ago our forefather brought forth upon this planet the spark of life. *(SOUND CUE #13B)*

(He is drowned out by THUNDER. When the thunder stops the FORTUNE TELLER is seen standing beside him. The BROADCAST OFFICIAL disappears. SABINA crosses to below bench, then crosses up Left Center.) *(LIGHT CUE #9)*

FORTUNE TELLER:

Antrobus, there's not a minute to be lost. Don't you see the four lights on the weather signal? Take your family into that boat at the end of the pier.

ANTROBUS:

(Crosses up Center)

My family? I have no family. Maggie! Maggie! They won't come.

FORTUNE TELLER:

They'll come.—Antrobus! Take these animals into that boat with you. All of them,—two of each kind.

SABINA:

(Crossing Right to ANTROBUS)

George, what's the matter with you? This is just a storm like any other storm.

ANTROBUS:

(Crossing up Left, calling)

Maggie!

SABINA:

Stay with me, we'll go—

(Losing conviction)

This is just another thunderstorm,—isn't **it?**

(Crossing to FORTUNE TELLER)

Isn't it?

ANTROBUS:
(Calling up Left)
Maggie!!!

(MRS. ANTROBUS *appears beside him with* GLADYS *from up Left.*)

MRS. ANTROBUS:
(Matter-of-fact)
Here I am and here's Gladys.

(SABINA *crosses down Right.*)

ANTROBUS:
Where've you been? Where have you been? Quick, we're going into that boat out there.
MRS. ANTROBUS:
I know we are. But I haven't found Henry.
(She wanders off up Right into the darkness calling "Henry.")

(FORTUNE TELLER *crosses to* ANTROBUS *and* GLADYS.)

SABINA:
(Sitting on bench. Low urgent babbling, only occasionally raising her voice)
I don't believe it. I don't believe it's anything at all. I've seen hundreds of storms like this.
FORTUNE TELLER:
(Pushing ANTROBUS to platform and ramp)
There's not a moment to be lost. Go push the animals along before you. Start a new world. Begin again.
(LIGHT CUE #10)
SABINA:
Esmeralda! George! Tell me,—is it really serious?

(GLADYS *starts down ramp.*)

ANTROBUS:
(Suddenly very busy starting on platform, working slowly down ramp)

Elephants first. Gently, gently.—Look where you're going.

> (FORTUNE TELLER *crosses stage Left to Right,*
> *watching* ANTROBUS *as he descends ramp.)*

GLADYS:
> *(Leaning over the ramp and striking an animal in*
> *the back. Bingo calling is heard)*

Stop it or you'll be left behind!

ANTROBUS:
Is the kangaroo there? *There* you are! Take those
turtles in your pouch, will you?
> *(To some other animals, pointing to his shoulder)*

Here! You jump up here. You'll be trampled on.

> (MRS. ANTROBUS *enters from up Right and crosses*
> *to up Left.)*

GLADYS:
> *(To her father, pointing below at the Right aisle)*

Papa, look—the snakes!

MRS. ANTROBUS:
I can't find Henry. Hen-ry. *(Exits up Left.)*

ANTROBUS:
Go along. Go along. Climb on their backs.—
> *(In aisle Right)*

Wolves! Jackals,—whatever you are,—tend to your
own business!

GLADYS:
> *(Pointing, tenderly)*

Papa,—look.

SABINA:
> *(Rise)*

Mr. Antrobus—take me with you.
> (ANTROBUS *crosses to Center on ramp)*

Don't leave me here. I'll work. I'll help. I'll do anything.
> *(Crosses down Left onto platform.)*

> (TWO CONVEENERS *appear up Left, crossing to*
> *Right. First one picks up banner down Left; car-*
> *ries it off.)*

(Stop bingo calling.)
2ND CONVEENER:
—George! What are you scared of—George!
(Imitating ANTROBUS)
Maggie, Maggie, where's my umbrella?
1ST CONVEENER:
Fellas, it looks like rain.
George, setting up for Barnum and Bailey.

(2ND CONVEENER crosses down Right; picks up banner; carries it off.)

GLADYS: *(Stop SOUND to out.)*
(At head of aisle) *(LIGHTNING flashes.)*
Mama! Papa! Hurry. The pier's cracking!
ANTROBUS:
Come on now, Maggie,—the pier's going to break any minute.
MRS. ANTROBUS:
(Crossing to up Center above bench)
I'm not going a step without Henry. Henry! Cain! Cain!
HENRY:
(Dashes into the stage from up Right and joins his mother up Center)
HENRY:
Here I am, Mama.
MRS. ANTROBUS:
Thank God! *(She embraces him.)*
HENRY:
I didn't think you wanted me.
(He hides his head on her arm.)
MRS. ANTROBUS: *(LIGHT CUE #10A)*
Now, come quick!
(She pushes him down before her onto the ramp into aisle.)
SABINA:
(All the ANTROBUSES are now in the theatre aisle. SABINA stands at the top of the ramp)
Mrs. Antrobus, take me. Don't you remember me? I'll work. I'll help. Don't leave me here!

MRS. ANTROBUS:
(Impatiently, but as though it were of no impor-
tance)
All right. There's a lot of work to be done. Only hurry
FORTUNE TELLER:
(Now dominating the stage. To SABINA with a
grim smile)
Back to the kitchen with you.
SABINA:
(Top of the ramp. To FORTUNE TELLER)
I don't know why my life's always being interrupted—
jus! when everything's going fine!!
(She opens her umbrella and runs down the ramp
and follows up the aisle.) (LIGHT CUE #11)
(SOUND CUE #14)
(Now the CONVEENERS emerge and doing a ser-
pentine dance on the stage. They jeer at the FOR-
TUNE TELLER, who mounts the bench, watching
the family running up the aisle)
(A CONVEENER and a MAJORETTE lead the parade
dancing; they dance above bench to Left Center,
then front of bench to Right Center)
(Following them another COUPLE (man and
woman) in a close embrace and with long steps
cross below bench to Left Center. They are fol-
lowed by a CONVEENER carrying a banner, holding
it as a canopy over their heads)
(A CONVEENER and another MAJORETTE follow,
crossing above bench to up Left Center)
(A CONVEENER with a BOY on his shoulders and
carrying a banner follows)
(TWO CONVEENERS leaning against each other fol-
low. ALL carry various noise-makers in addition
to their shouting and calling)
(Off stage Right FOUR WOMEN and a MAN scream
and laugh along with the parade.)

CONVEENERS:
Get a canoe—there's not a minute to be lost! Tell me
my future, Mrs. Croaker.

FORTUNE TELLER:
Paddle in the water, boys—enjoy yourselves.
BINGO ANNOUNCER:
  (From the Bingo Parlor)
A-nine; A-nine. C-twenty-four. C-twenty-four.
FORTUNE TELLER:
Go back and climb on your roofs. Put rags in the cracks under your doors—nothing will keep out the flood. You've had your chance. You've had your day. You've failed. You've lost.
  (She speaks at the DANCERS clear from front of bench. Shading her eyes and looking out to sea)
They're safe.
  (The PARADERS stop moving and speaking)
George Antrobus! Think it over! A new world to make.
Think it over!   *(SOUND CUE #14A)*

FAST CURTAIN

ACT THREE

During the intermission the two men who as Conveeners *set up the rails, standards and rope, appear as*
Theatre Ushers *and take down what was set.
When finished they exit up the aisle into the audience.*
*Just before the Curtain rises a sound is heard from
the stage: a cracked BUGLE CALL.*
*The Curtain rises on almost total darkness. Al-
most all the flats composing the walls of* Mr. Antrobus's *house, as of Act One, are up, but they
lean helter-skelter against one another, leaving
irregular gaps. The flat is missing in the back wall,
leaving the frame of the window crazily out of
line. At Right Center is a trap door. Off stage,
back Right, some red Roman fire is burning.*

(LIGHT CUE #1)

*The Hamlet chair is still down Right, also the
bench below pagoda; hassock is Right of trap
Right Center; sofa above trap; clothes-tree leaning against door Left; round table against base of
tree and to its Right; rocking-chair above table
and facing upstage; armchair against table and to
its Left; one fire dog is standing and the other
down. Chandelier is on the floor Center. Platform
back of Center outside.*
The BUGLE CALL is repeated. Enter Sabina
*from up Left corner. She is dressed as a Napo-
leonic camp follower, "La fille du regiment," in
begrimed reds and blues.*

Sabina:
Mrs. Antrobus! Gladys! Where are you?

93

(Crossing to Center)

The war's over. The war's over. You can come out. The peace treaty's been signed.   *(LIGHT CUE #2)* Where are they?—Hmpf! Are they dead, too? Mrs. Annnntrobus! Glaaaadus!

(Crossing up Right to stairs)

Mr. Antrobus'll be here this afternoon. I just saw him downtown. Huuuurry and put things in order. He says that now that the war's over we'll all have to settle down and be perfect.

(Enter FITZPATRICK from down Left. He tries to interrupt SABINA)

FITZPATRICK:

Miss Somerset.

SABINA:

They

(Crossing to door Right)

may be hiding out in the back—

FITZPATRICK:

Miss Somerset! We have to stop a moment.

SABINA:

What's the matter?

FITZPATRICK:

There's an explanation we have to make to the audience.—Lights, please.

(ANTROBUS enters from down Left)

(To ANTROBUS)   *(LIGHT CUE #3)*

Will you explain the matter to the audience?

(A GIRL ASSISTANT STAGE MANAGER enters from down Left with script and numerals. MR. TREMAYNE enters from down Left—crosses to Left Center. SABINA sits hassock Right Center. The LIGHTS go up. We now see that a platform or elevated runway has been erected at back of the Antrobus house. From its extreme Right and Left ends ladder-like steps descend to the floor of the stage.)

ANTROBUS:

Ladies and gentlemen, an unfortunate accident has taken place back stage.

94

(Two colored girls enter—Hester from up Left corner and Ivy from down Right—crosses to Sabina)

Perhaps
(Looking at Sabina)
I should say *another* unfortunate accident.

SABINA:
I'm sorry. I'm sorry.

(Two Men enter from up Left onto platform at back. Two Men and Two Women enter from down Right. Fred Bailey comes down Right aisle to ramp. Two Men and One Woman enter up Right onto steps of pagoda.)

ANTROBUS:
The management feels, in fact we all feel that you are due an apology. And now we have to ask your indulgence for the most serious mishap of all. Seven of our actors have—have been taken ill. Apparently, it was something they ate. I'm not exactly clear what happened.
(All the Actors start to talk at once. Antrobus raises his hand)
Now, now—not all at once. Fitz, do you know what it was?

FITZPATRICK:
Why, it's perfectly clear. These seven actors had dinner together, and they ate something that disagreed with them.

SABINA:
Disagreed with them!!! They have ptomaine poisoning. They're in Bellevue Hospital this very minute in agony. They're having their stomachs pumped out this very minute, in perfect agony.

ANTROBUS:
Fortunately, we've just heard they'll all recover.

SABINA:
It'll be a miracle if they do, a downright miracle. It was the lemon meringue pie.

TREMAYNE:
It was the fish—
WOMAN:
   (Down Right)   } (Together)
It was the canned tomatoes—
TREMAYNE:
It was the fish.
SABINA:
It was the lemon meringue pie. I saw it with my own
eyes; it had blue mould all over the bottom of it.

   (FITZPATRICK *crosses up.*)

ANTROBUS:
Whatever it was, they're in no condition to take part
in this performance. Naturally, we haven't enough un-
derstudies to fill all those roles; but we do have a number of splendid volunteers who have kindly consented
to help us out.
   (HESTER *and* IVY *cross down Left.* BAILEY *up
   ramp to down Left)*
These friends have watched our rehearsals, and they
assure me that they know the lines and the business
very well. Let me introduce them to you—my dresser,
Mr. Tremayne,—himself a distinguished Shakespear-
ean actor for many years;
   (TREMAYNE *steps down; takes deep bow)*
Miss Somerset's maid, Ivy; our wardrobe mistress,
Hester; and Fred Bailey, captain of the ushers in this
theatre.
   (BAILEY *swallows with fear.*
   HESTER *and* IVY *bow modestly)*
Now this scene takes place near the end of the act. And
I'm sorry to say we'll need a short rehearsal, just a
short run-through. And as some of it takes place in the
auditorium, we'll have to keep the curtain up. Those of
you who wish can go out in the lobby and smoke some
more. The rest of you can listen to us, or—or just talk
quietly among yourselves, as you choose. Thank you.
   (Crossing up Center to Left of sofa)
Now will you take it over, Mr. Fitzpatrick?

FITZPATRICK:

(Crossing up down Center—places script on floor)
Thank you.—Now for those of you who are listening
perhaps I should explain that at the end of this act, the
men have come back from the war and the family's
settled down in the house. And the author wants to
show the hours of the night passing by over their
heads, and the planets crossing the sky—uh—over their
heads. And he says—this is hard to explain—

(Look to ANTROBUS*)*
that each of the hours of the night is a philosopher, or
a great thinker. Eleven o'clock, for instance, is Aristotle. And nine o'clock is Spinoza. Like that. I don't
suppose it means anything. It's just a kind of poetic
effect.

SABINA:

Not mean anything! Why, it certainly does. Twelve
o'clock goes by saying those wonderful things. I think
it means that when people are asleep they have all those
lovely thoughts, much better than when they're awake.

IVY:

(Steps down)
Excuse me, I think it means,—excuse me, Mr. Fitzpatrick—

SABINA:

What were you going to say, Ivy?

IVY:

Mr. Fitzpatrick, you let my father come to a rehearsal;
and my father's a Baptist minister, and he said that the
author meant that—just like the hours and stars go by
over our heads at night, in the same way the ideas and
thoughts of the great men are in the air around us all
the time and they're working on us, even when we
don't know it.

(ALL react to the explanation.)

FITZPATRICK:

Well, well, maybe that's it. Thank you, Ivy. Anyway,—
the hours of the night are philosophers. My friends,
are you ready?

*(ASSISTANT STAGE MANAGER crosses back to hand
out numerals)*

Ivy, can you be eleven o'clock? "This good estate of
the mind possessing its object in energy we call divine—" Aristotle.

IVY:

Yes, sir. I know that and I know twelve o'clock
(Suggests numeral)
and I know nine o'clock.

FITZPATRICK:

Twelve o'clock? Mr. Tremayne, the Bible.
(Numeral to him.)

TREMAYNE:

Yes.

FITZPATRICK:

Ten o'clock? Hester,—Plato?
*(Numeral to her. She nods eagerly. The GROUP
up Right and down Right exit)*
Nine o'clock, Spinoza,—Fred?
(Numeral to him.)

BAILEY:

Yes, *sir.*

FITZPATRICK:

(Strikes his forehead)
The planets!! We forgot all about the planets.

SABINA:

O my God! The planets! Are they sick too?

(ACTORS nod.)

FITZPATRICK:

Ladies and gentlemen, the planets are singers. Of
course, we can't replace them, so you'll have to imagine
them singing in this scene. Saturn sings from the orchestra pit down here. The Moon is way up there. And
Mars, with a red lantern in his hand, stands in the aisle
over there—Tz-tz-tz. It's too bad; it all makes a very
fine effect. However! Ready—
(Crosses to BAILEY)
—nine o'clock: Spinoza.

98   ACT III

BAILEY:

(Walking slowly across the stage, Left to Right, talking softly)

"After experience had taught me that the common occurrences of daily life are vain and futile—"

FITZPATRICK:

Louder, Fred. "And I saw that all the objects of my desire and fear—"

(ANTROBUS steps down, walks BAILEY to Right, then hold at proscenium.)

BAILEY:

"And I saw that all the objects of my desire and fear were in themselves nothing good nor bad save insofar as the mind was affected by them—"

(BAILEY exits Right below set.)

FITZPATRICK:

Do you know the rest? All right. Ten o'clock. Hester. Plato.

HESTER:

(Crossing from Left to Right)

"Then tell me, O Critias, how shall a man choose the ruler that he is willing should rule over him? Will he not—"

FITZPATRICK:

Thank you. Skip to the end, Hester.

HESTER:

"—can be multiplied a thousand fold in its effects among the citizens."

(Exits Right below set.)

FITZPATRICK:

Thank you.—Aristotle, Ivy?

IVY:

(Crossing Left to Right)

"This good estate of the mind possessing its object in energy we call divine. This we mortals have occasion-

(TREMAYNE starts crossing Right slowly)

ally and it is this energy which is pleasantest and best. But God has it always. It is wonderful in us; but in Him how much more wonderful."

(Exits Right below set.)

(ANTROBUS *exits Right after* IVY.)

FITZPATRICK:
(Crossing Left)
Midnight.
(Not seeing him—shouting)
Midnight, Mr. Tremayne.
TREMAYNE:
Yes!
FITZPATRICK:
That's right,—you've done it before.—All right, everybody.
(SABINA *rises; crosses up Left. Exits*)
You know what you have to do.—
(To the ASSISTANT *who exits down Left)*
Lower the curtain. House lights. Act Three of *The Skin of Our Teeth.*   *(LIGHT CUE #4)*
(As the Curtain descends he is heard saying:)
                                        (BUGLE CALL)
You volunteers, just wear what you have on.
Don't try to put on the costumes today.

(The Act begins again. Curtain rises. The BUGLE CALL again. Enter SABINA *from up Left corner)*

SABINA: *(LIGHT CUE #5)*
Mrs. Antrobus! Gladys!
Where are you?
(Crossing Center)
The war's over—
(To audience)
You've heard all this—
(She gabbles the main points)
(Crossing to steps up Right)
Where—are—they? Are—they—dead, too, etcetera.
I—just—saw—Mr.—Antrobus—downtown, etcetera.
(Slowing up:)
He says that now that the war's over we'll all have to settle down and be perfect.   *(LIGHT CUE #6)*
They may be hiding out in the back somewhere. Mrs. An-tro-bus.

(She wanders off Right below set. It has grown lighter.)

MRS. ANTROBUS:

(The trap door Right Center is cautiously raised and MRS. ANTROBUS emerges waist-high and listens. She is disheveled and worn; she wears a tattered dress and a shawl half covers her head. She talks down through the trap door)

It's getting light. There's still something burning over there—Newark, or Jersey City. What? Yes, I could swear I heard someone moving about up here. But I can't see anybody. I say: I can't see anybody.

(She starts to move about the stage, crossing Right.)

GLADYS:

(GLADYS' head appears at the trap door. She is holding a baby)

Oh, Mama. Be careful.

MRS. ANTROBUS:

Now, Gladys, you stay out of sight.

(Crossing up Center to window.)

GLADYS:

Well, let me stay here just a minute. I want the baby to get some of this fresh air.

(Opens blanket over baby's face.)

MRS. ANTROBUS:

All right, but keep your eyes open.

(Picks up hoe at window—crosses down Center)

I'll see what I can find. I'll have a good hot plate of soup for you before you can say Jack Robinson.

(Crosses up to window. Peeks out of window)

Gladys Antrobus! Do you know what I think I see? There's old Mr. Hawkins sweeping the sidewalk in front of his A. and P. store. Sweeping it with a broom. Why, he must have gone crazy, like the others.

(Look off Left between flats)

$\qquad$ *(PROPERTY CUE #1)*

I see some other people moving about, too.

GLADYS:

Mama, come back, come back.

MRS. ANTROBUS:
> *(Returns to trap door and listens; then crossing up to window)*

Gladys, there's something in the air. Everybody's movement's sort of different. I see some women walking right out in the middle of the street.

SABINA:
> *(Distant. Calling by crossing back stage under scenery)*

Mrs. An-tro-bus!

MRS. ANTROBUS *and* GLADYS:
What's that?!!

SABINA:
> *(Calling)*

Glaaaadys! Mrs. An-tro-bus!

MRS. ANTROBUS:
Gladys, that's Sabina's voice as sure as I live.—Sabina! Sabina!—Are you alive?!!

SABINA:
> *(Enters from up Left corner)*

Of course I'm alive.
> *(Crossing Center)*

How've you girls been?
> *(MRS. ANTROBUS crosses to her)*

—Don't try and kiss me. I never want to kiss another human being as long as I live. Sh-sh, there's nothing to get emotional about. Pull yourself together, the war's over. Take a deep breath,—the war's over.

MRS. ANTROBUS:
The war's over!! I don't believe you. I don't believe you. I can't believe you.

GLADYS:
Mama!

SABINA:
What's that?   *(LIGHT CUE #7)*

MRS. ANTROBUS:
That's Gladys's baby. I don't believe you. Gladys, Sabina says the war's over. Oh, Sabina. *(Quiet weeping.)*

SABINA:
> *(Crossing to her—leaning over the baby)*

Goodness! Are there any babies left in the world! Can it *see?* And can it cry and everything?

(MRS. ANTROBUS *crosses to armchair Left Center.)*

GLADYS:
Yes, he can. He notices everything very well.
SABINA:
Where on earth did you get it? Oh, I won't ask.—Lord, I've lived all these seven years around camp and I've forgotten how to behave.—Now we've got to think about the men coming home.—
    (Crossing to her)
Mrs. Antrobus, go and wash your face, I'm ashamed of you. Put your best clothes on. Mr. Antrobus'll be here this afternoon. I just saw him downtown.
MRS. ANTROBUS *and* GLADYS:
    (Together)
He's alive!! Sabina, you're not joking?
MRS. ANTROBUS:
He'll be here?! And Henry?
SABINA:
    (Dryly)
Yes, Henry's alive, too, that's what they say. Now don't stop to talk. Get yourselves fixed up. Gladys, you look terrible.
    (GLADYS *exits down trap)*
Have you any decent clothes?
MRS. ANTROBUS:
    (Crossing to trap)
Yes, I've been saving something to wear for this very day. But, Sabina,—who won the war?
SABINA:
Don't stop now,—just wash your face.
    (A WHISTLE sounds in the distance twice)
Oh, my God, what's that silly little noise?
MRS. ANTROBUS:
Why, it sounds like—it sounds like what used to be the noon whistle at the shoe-polish factory.
    (Exits down trap.)

SABINA:

That's what it is. Seems to me like peacetime's coming along pretty fast—shoe polish!

GLADYS:

(Coming up from trap high enough to show head) Sabina, how soon after peacetime begins does the milkman start coming to the door?

SABINA:

As soon as he catches a cow. Give him time to catch a cow, dear.

(Exit GLADYS to trap. SABINA takes off her coat) Shoe polish! My, I'd forgotten what peacetime was like.

(She shakes her head, places coat on. Left end of sofa, throws knapsack on bench up Right, then sits down on sofa by the trap door and starts talking down the hole) (LIGHT CUE #8)

Mrs. Antrobus, guess what I saw Mr. Antrobus doing this morning at dawn. He was tacking up a piece of paper on the door of the Town Hall. You'll die when you hear: it was a recipe for grass soup, for a grass soup that doesn't give the diarrhea. Mr. Antrobus is still thinking up new things.—He told me to give you his love. He's got all sorts of ideas for peacetime, he says. No more laziness and idiocy, he says. And oh, yes! Where are his books? What? Well, pass them up. The first thing he wants to see are his books. He says if you've burnt those books, or if the rats have eaten them, he says it isn't worthwhile starting over again. Everybody's going to be beautiful, he says, and diligent, and very intelligent.

(A hand reaches up with one volume)

What language is that? Pugh, German!

(Throws book on floor Left of sofa)

And he's got such plans for you, Mrs. Antrobus. You're going to study history and algebra—and so are Gladys and I—and philosophy. You should hear him talk:

(Taking two more volumes)

Well, these are in English, anyway.

(Throws books on floor Left of sofa)

—To hear him talk, seems like he expects you to be a combination, Mrs. Antrobus, of a saint and a college professor, and a dance hall hostess, if you know what I mean.

(She is lying on the sofa; one elbow bent, her cheek on her hand, meditatively takes her revolver from holster)

Yes, peace will be here before we know it. In a week or two we'll be asking the Perkinses in for a quiet evening of bridge. We'll turn on the radio and hear how to be big successes with a new tooth paste. We'll trot down to the movies and see how girls with wax faces live—

(Aims gun)

all *that* will begin again.

(Shoots in the air)

Oh, Mrs. Antrobus, God forgive me but I enjoyed the war. Everybody's at their best in wartime. I'm sorry it's over. And, oh, I forgot! Mr. Antrobus sent you another message—can you hear me?—

(Enter HENRY from up Left corner, blackened and sullen. He is wearing torn overalls, but has one gawdy admiral's epaulette hanging by a thread from his right shoulder, and there are vestiges of gold and scarlet braid running down his left trouser leg. He listens to SABINA—crosses into Center)

Listen! Henry's never to put foot in this house again, he says. He'll kill Henry on sight, if he sees him.

You don't know about Henry??? Well, where have you been? What? Well, Henry rose right to the top. Top of *what?* Listen, I'm telling you. Henry rose from corporal to captain, to major, to general.—I don't know how to say it, but the enemy is *Henry;* Henry *is* the enemy. Everybody knows that.

HENRY:

He'll kill me, will he?

SABINA:

Who are *you?* I'm not afraid of you. The war's over.

HENRY:

I'll kill him so fast. I've spent seven years trying to find him; the others I killed were just substitutes.

SABINA:

> *(Turns to him; rises; crosses to Right end of sofa)*

Goodness! It's Henry!—

> *(He makes an angry gesture. She puts hand on gun holster)*

Oh, I'm not afraid of you. The war's over, Henry Antrobus, and you're not any more important than any other unemployed. You go away and hide yourself, until we calm your father down.

HENRY:

> *(Crossing into sofa)*

The first thing to do is to burn up those old books; it's the ideas he gets out of those old books that—that makes the whole world so you can't live in it.

> *(Stamps on books.)*

SABINA:

You leave those books alone!! Mr. Antrobus is looking forward to them a-special.

> *(He reels forward and starts kicking the books about, but suddenly falls down in a sitting position above armchair Left Center)*
>
> *(LIGHT CUE #9)*

Gracious sakes, Henry, you're so tired you can't stand up.

> *(He rises)*

Your mother and sister'll be here in a minute and we'll think what to do about you.

HENRY:

What did they ever care about me?

> *(Throws off helmet up Center.)*

SABINA:

There's that old whine again.

> (HENRY *crosses down Left below furniture)*

All you people think you're not loved enough, nobody loves you. Well, you start being lovable and we'll love you.

HENRY:

> *(Outraged)*

I don't want anybody to love me.

SABINA:

Then stop talking about it all the time.

HENRY:
I *never* talk about it. The last thing I want is anybody to pay any attention to me.
SABINA:
I can hear it behind every word you say.
HENRY:
I want everybody to hate me.
SABINA:
Yes, you've decided that's second best, but it's still the same thing.—
    (Calling down—Right of trap)
Mrs. Antrobus! Henry's here. He's so tired he can't stand up.

    (MRS. ANTROBUS *and* GLADYS, *with her baby, emerge. After they are up,* SABINA *closes trap door.)*   *(LIGHT CUE #10)*

MRS. ANTROBUS *and* GLADYS: *(Together)*
Henry! Henry! Henry!
    (MRS. ANTROBUS *crosses to Center.* GLADYS *crosses to Right of* MRS. ANTROBUS.)

MRS. ANTROBUS:
Henry!
HENRY:
    (Glaring at them)
Have you anything to eat?

    (GLADYS *crosses up to sofa.)*

MRS. ANTROBUS:
Yes, I have, Henry.
    (Crossing to fireplace to get potatoes)
I've been saving it for this very day,—two good baked potatoes. One of them's for your father.
    (HENRY *rushes to her, grabs the potatoes from her —sits armchair eating one)*
Henry!! Give me that other potato back this minute.
SABINA:
    (Sidles up behind him and snatches the other po tato away. Giving MRS. ANTROBUS *the potato)*

He's so dog-tired he doesn't know what he's doing.

MRS. ANTROBUS:

Now you just rest there until I can get your room ready. Eat that potato good and slow, so you can get all the nourishment out of it.

HENRY:

You all might as well know right now that I haven't come back here to live.

MRS. ANTROBUS:

Sh—

> *(Picks up* SABINA'S *coat from sofa, crosses to him —places coat around him)*

I'll put this coat over you. Your room's hardly damaged at all. Your football trophies are a little tarnished, but Sabina and I will polish them up tomorrow.

HENRY:

Did you hear me? I don't live here. I don't belong to anybody.

MRS. ANTROBUS:

Why, how can you say a thing like that? You certainly do belong right here. Where else would you want to go? Your forehead's feverish, Henry, seems to me.

> *(Taking his gun from holster)*

You'd better give me that gun, Henry. You won't need that any more.

GLADYS:

> *(Whisper)*

Look, he's fallen asleep already, with his potato half-chewed.

SABINA:

Puh! The terror of the world.

MRS. ANTROBUS:

Sabina, you mind your own business, and start putting the room to rights.

> *(*HENRY *has turned his face to the back of the chair.* MRS. ANTROBUS *gingerly puts gun in pocket. She crosses to door Left, takes clothestree from door, places it up Left corner, then she moves the table to Right of chair* HENRY *is in.* GLADYS crosses to hassock Right Center, sits holding baby.*

SABINA *has found a rope hanging from the ceiling.
Grunting, she hangs all her weight on it, and as she
pulls, the walls begin to move into their right
places.)*   *(FLY CUE #1)*

SABINA:
That's all we do—always beginning again!
Over and over again.
Always beginning again.
    *(She gives the rope one good tug and then stops.
    Meditatively:)*
How do we know that it'll be any better than before?
Why do we go on pretending? Some day the whole
earth's going to have to turn cold anyway, and until
that time all these other things'll be happening again:
it will be more wars and more walls of ice and floods
and earthquakes.
MRS. ANTROBUS:
Sabina!! Stop arguing and go on with your work.
SABINA:
All right. I'll go on just out of *habit,* but I won't believe in it.
MRS. ANTROBUS:
    (Aroused, takes the rope from SABINA. SABINA
    crosses down to sofa—sits on head of sofa)
Now, Sabina. I've let you talk long enough. I don't
want to hear any more of it. Do I have to explain to
you what everybody knows,—everybody who keeps a
home going? Do I have to say to you what nobody
should ever *have* to say, because they can read it in
each other's eyes?
Now listen to me:
    *(*MRS. ANTROBUS *pulls on the rope and the house
    completely rights itself)*
I could live for seventy years   *(FLY CUE #2)*
in a cellar and make soup out   *(LIGHT CUE #11)*
of grass and bark, without ever   *(FLY CUE #3)*
doubting that this world has a work to do and will do it.
Do you hear me?

SABINA:
(Frightened)
Yes, Mrs. Antrobus.
MRS. ANTROBUS:
Sabina, do you see this house,—216 Cedar Street,—do
you see it?
SABINA:
Yes, Mrs. Antrobus.
MRS. ANTROBUS:
Well, just to have known this house—is to have seen
the idea of what this world can do some day—can do
some day, if we keep our wits about us.
Too many people have suffered and died in order to
make my children rich, for us to start reneging now.
So we'll go on putting this house to rights. Now, Sa-
bina, go and see what you can do in the kitchen.
(Picks up books from floor—places them on table.)
SABINA:
Kitchen! Why is it that, however far I go away,
(Crossing Right)
I always find myself back in the kitchen? *(Exits Right.)*
(FLY CUE #4)
MRS. ANTROBUS: *(LIGHT CUE #12)*
*(Relaxes and says with a smile: Starts to move
sofa up Center. GLADYS helps her)*
Goodness gracious, wouldn't you know my father was
a parson? It was just like I heard his own voice speak-
ing, and he's been dead five thousand years.
(HENRY grunts in his sleep)
There! I've gone and almost waked Henry up.
HENRY:
(Talking in his sleep, indistinctly)
Fellows— What have they done for us?—Blocked our
way at every step. Kept everything in their own hands.
And you've stood it.
When are you going to wake up?
MRS. ANTROBUS:
(Crosses to him; tucks coat over shoulders)
Sh, Henry. Go to sleep. Go to sleep.
*(Moves rocking-chair from Left Center to Right
of table)*

Go to sleep.—Well, that looks better.

(Places books from table into bag on arm of rock-
ing-chair)

Now let's go and help Sabina.

GLADYS:

(Crossing to door Right)

Mama, I'm going out into the back yard and hold the
baby right up in the air. And show him that we don't
have to be afraid any more. *(Exits Right.)*

(HENRY grunts in his sleep.)
(MRS. ANTROBUS glances at HENRY; exits Right.)
(ANTROBUS is heard whistling off Left as he ap-
proaches door Left. HENRY thrashes about in his
sleep. Enter ANTROBUS, his arms full of bundles.
He has a slight limp. He is wearing an overcoat
too long for him, its skirts trailing on the ground.
ANTROBUS crosses down to down Right. He lets his
bundles fall on chair down Right and stands look-
ing about. Presently his attention is fixed on
HENRY, whose words grow clearer. ANTROBUS
snaps out his revolver as he hears HENRY.)

HENRY:

Okay! What have you got to lose? What have they
done for us? That's right—nothing. Tear everything
down. I don't care what you smash. We'll begin again
and we'll show 'em.

(ANTROBUS holds his revolver pointing downwards.
With his back towards the audience, he moves
toward the footlights. HENRY's voice grows louder
and he wakes with a start. They stare at one an-
other. Then HENRY sits up quickly. He throws off
coat, reaches for his revolver, finds it gone—rises
quickly and backs away into the up Left corner)

All right! Do something.

(Pause)

Don't think I'm afraid of you, either. All right, do
what you were going to do. Do it.

(Furiously)

Shoot me, I tell you.

(Antrobus points gun down)

You don't have to think I'm any relation of yours. I haven't got any father or any mother, or brothers or sisters. And I don't want any. I'm alone, and that's all I want to be: alone. And what's more I haven't got anybody over me; and I never will have. So you can shoot me.

ANTROBUS:

You're the last person I wanted to see. The sight of you dries up all my plans and hopes. I wish I were back at war still, because it's easier to fight you than to live with you. War's a pleasure—do you hear me?—War's a pleasure compared to what faces us now:

(Crossing up Center to window slowly)

trying to build up a peacetime with you in the middle of it.

HENRY:

I'm not going to be a part of any peacetime of yours. I'm going a long way from here and make my own world that's fit for a man to live in. Where a man can be free, and have a chance, and do what he wants to do in his own way.

ANTROBUS:

(His attention arrested; he throws his revolver out of the window; thoughtfully)

Henry, let's try again.

HENRY:

Try what? Living *here?*—Speaking polite downtown to all the old men like you?

(Antrobus turns away)

Standing like a sheep at the street-corner until the red light turns to green? Being a good boy and a good sheep, like all the stinking ideas you get out of your books.

(Antrobus turns to Henry)

Oh, no. I'll make a world, and I'll show you.

ANDROBUS:

(Hard)

How can you make a world for people to live in, unless you've first put order in yourself? Mark my words: I shall continue fighting you until my last breath as long as you mix up your idea of liberty with your idea of hogging everything for yourself. I shall have no pity on you. I shall pursue you to the far corners of the earth. You and I want the same thing; but until you think of it as something that everyone has a right to, you are my deadly enemy and I will destroy you.—I hear your mother's voice in the kitchen. Have you seen her?

HENRY:

> *(Crossing into back of chair Left Center)*

I have no mother. Get it into your head. I don't belong here. I have nothing to do here. I have no home.

ANTROBUS:

Then why did you come here? With the whole world to choose from, why did you come to this one place: 216 Cedar Street, Excelsior, New Jersey—

> *(HENRY turns away)*

Well?

HENRY:

> *(Crossing down Left)*

What if I did? What if I wanted to look at it once more, to see if—

ANTROBUS:

> *(Turns—crossing down Right)*

Oh, you're related, all right— When your mother comes in you must behave yourself.

> *(Turns to HENRY)*

Do you hear me?

HENRY:

> *(Wildly)*

What is this?—*must behave* yourself. Don't you say *must* to me.

ANTROBUS:

Quiet!

HENRY:

Nobody can say *must* to me.

> *(Crossing up Center slowly—stalking)*

All my life everybody's been crossing me,—everybody, everything, all of you. I'm going to be free, even if I have to kill half the world for it.

> *(SABINA and MRS. ANTROBUS enter from Right)*

Right now, too. Let me get my hands on his throat. I'll show him.

(He advances toward ANTROBUS. *Suddenly* SA-BINA *jumps between them and calls out in her own person:* MRS. ANTROBUS *pulls* ANTROBUS *away. He turns up stage.* MRS. ANTROBUS *to his Right.* HENRY *backs away up Center.* SABINA *to his Right.)*

SABINA:

Stop! Stop! Don't play this scene. You know what happened last night. Stop the play.

(The MEN *fall back, panting.* HENRY *covers his face with his hands)*

Ladies and gentlemen, I forbid these men to play this scene. Last night this boy here almost strangled him. He becomes a regular savage. Stop it!

HENRY:

It's true. I'm sorry. I don't know what comes over me. I have nothinng against him personally. I respect him very much— I—I admire him. But something comes over me. It's like I become fifteen years old again. I— I—listen: my own father used to whip me and lock me up every Saturday night. I never had enough to eat. He never let me have enough money to buy decent clothes. I was ashamed to go downtown. I never could go to the dances. My father and my uncle put rules in the way of everything I wanted to do. They tried to prevent my living at all.

(Turns away)

—I'm sorry. I'm sorry.

MRS. ANTROBUS:

(Quickly)

No, go on. Finish what you were saying. Say it all.

HENRY:

In this scene it's as though I were back in High School again. It's like I had some big emptiness inside me,— the emptiness of being hated and blocked at every turn. And the emptiness fills up with the one thought that you have to strike and fight and kill. Listen, it's as though you have to kill somebody else so as not to end up killing yourself.

SABINA:

That's not true. I knew your father and your uncle and your mother. You imagined all that. Why, they did everything they could for you. How can you say things like that? They didn't lock you up.

HENRY:

They did. They did. They wished I hadn't been born

SABINA:

That's not true!

ANTROBUS:

(In his own person, with self-condemnation, but cold and proud—turns to them)

Wait a minute. I have something to say, too. It's not wholly his fault that he wants to strangle me in this scene. It's my fault, too. He wouldn't feel that way unless there were something in me that reminded him of all that. He talks about emptiness. Well, there's an emptiness in me, too. Yes—work, work, work,—that's all I do. I've ceased to *live*.

(Crossing down Right)

No wonder he feels that anger coming over him.

MRS. ANTROBUS:

There! At last you've said it.

SABINA:

We're all just as wicked as we can be, and that's the God's truth.

MRS. ANTROBUS:

(Nods a moment, then comes forward; quietly)

Come,

(Crossing to Right of SABINA)

come and put your head under some cold water.

SABINA:

(In a whisper)

I'll go with him. You have to go on with the play. I've known him a long while. Come with me, Henry.

(BOTH cross Right to door. MRS. ANTROBUS crosses up Center. HENRY starts out with SABINA, but turns at the exit and says to ANTROBUS:)

HENRY:

Thanks. Thanks for what you said. I'll be all right tomorrow. I won't lose control in that place, I promise.

> *(Exeunt* HENRY *and* SABINA*)*
> *(*ANTROBUS *crosses Left to door. Sets lock, closes door, and stands lost in thought.* MRS. ANTROBUS *takes chair from Left Center to Left of table.)*

MRS. ANTROBUS:
George, you're limping?
ANTROBUS:
Yes, a little. My old wound from the other war started smarting again.

> *(*MRS. ANTROBUS *takes coat from chair to sofa up Center)*

I can manage.
MRS. ANTROBUS:

> *(Looking out of the window)*

Some lights are coming on,—the first in seven years. People are walking up and down looking at them. Over in Hawkins' open lot they've built a bonfire to celebrate the peace. They're dancing around it like scarecrows.
ANTROBUS:
A bonfire!

> *(Crossing to window)*

As though they hadn't seen enough things burning.— Maggie,—the dog died?
MRS. ANTROBUS:
Oh, yes. Long ago. There are no dogs left in Excelsior.

> *(She crosses to him—they embrace)*

You're back again! All these years. I gave up counting on letters. The few that arrived were anywhere from six months to a year late.
ANTROBUS:
Yes, the ocean's full of letters, along with the other things.
MRS. ANTROBUS:
George, sit down, you're tired.
ANTROBUS:
No, you sit down. I'm tired but I'm restless.

> *(Suddenly, as she comes forward to chair Right of table)*

Maggie! I've lost it. I've lost it.

MRS. ANTROBUS:

(Sits chair Right of table)

What, George? What have you lost?

ANTROBUS:

The most important thing of all: **The desire to begin again**, to start building.

MRS. ANTROBUS:

Well, it will come back.

ANTROBUS:

(Above chair Left of table)

I've lost it.

(Crossing up Center near window)

This minute I feel like all those people dancing around the bonfire—just relief. Just the desire to settle down; to slip into the old grooves and keep the neighbors from walking over my lawn.—Hm.

(Takes off coat and holster—throws them on sofa, then crosses down to above table)

But during the war,—in the middle of all that blood and dirt and hot and cold—every day and night, I'd have moments, Maggie, when I *saw* the things that we could do when it was over. When you're at war you think about a better life; when you're at peace you think about a more comfortable one.

(Crossing down Left)

I've lost it. I feel sick and tired.

MRS. ANTROBUS:

Listen! The baby's crying.   *(LIGHT CUE #15)*

(She listens. Rises)

I hear Gladys talking. Probably she's quieting Henry again. George,

(Crosses Left to him)

while Gladys and I were living here—like moles, like rats, and when we were at our wits end to save the baby's life—the only thought we clung to was that you were going to bring something good out of this suffering. In the night, in the dark, we'd whisper about it, starving and sick.—Oh, George, you'll have to get it back again. Think! What else kept us alive all these years? Even now, it's not comfort we want. We can suffer whatever's necessary; only give us back that promise.

SABINA:

> (Enters with a lighted lamp from Right. Crosses Right Center)

Mrs. Antrobus—

MRS. ANTROBUS:

Yes, Sabina?

SABINA:

Will you need me?

MRS. ANTROBUS:

No, Sabina, you can go to bed.

> (To chair Right of table—sits.)

SABINA:

> (Crossing to above table—places lamp on table)

Mrs. Antrobus, if it's all right with you, I'd like to go to the bonfire and celebrate seeing the war's over. And Mrs. Antrobus, they've opened the Gem Movie Theatre and they're giving away a hand-painted soup tureen to every lady, and I thought one of us ought to go.

ANTROBUS:

Well, Sabina, I haven't any money. I haven't seen any money for quite a while.

SABINA:

Oh, you don't need money. They're taking anything you can give them. And I have some—some—Mrs. Antrobus, promise you won't tell anyone. It's a little against the law. But I'll give you some, too.

ANTROBUS:

What is it?

SABINA:

> (Step to him)

I'll give you some, too. Yesterday I picked up a lot of—of beef-cubes!

MRS. ANTROBUS:

> (Turns and says calmly)

But, Sabina, you know you ought to give that in to the Center downtown. They know who needs them most.

SABINA:

> (Outburst)

Mrs. Antrobus, I didn't make this war. I didn't **ask**

for it. And in my opinion, after anybody's gone through what we've gone through, they have a right to grab what they can find. You're a very nice man, Mr. Antrobus, but you'd have got on better in the world if you'd realized that dog-eat-dog was the rule in the beginning and always will be. And most of all now.

(In tears)

Oh, the world's an awful place,

(Turns away from him)

and you know it is. I used to think something could be done about it; but I know better now. I hate it. I hate it.

(She comes forward slowly and takes cubes from her handbag)

All right. All right. You can have them.

(Gives them to ANTROBUS, *then crosses to door Left.)*

ANTROBUS:

(Crossing to table—places cubes on table)

Thank you, Sabina.

SABINA:

(Crossing to him)

Can I have—can I have one to go to the movies?

*(*ANTROBUS *in silence gives her one)*

Thank you.

ANTROBUS:

Good night, Sabina.

SABINA:

Mr. Antrobus, don't mind what I say. I'm just an ordinary girl, you know what I mean, I'm just an ordinary girl. But you're a bright man, you're a very bright man, and of course you invented the alphabet and the wheel, and, my God, a lot of things—and if you've got any other plans, my God, don't let me upset them. Only every now and then I've got to go to the movies. I mean my nerves can't stand it. But if you have any ideas about improving the crazy old world, I'm really with you. I really am. Because it's—it's—Good night. *(She goes out Left.)*

ANTROBUS:

(Laughing softly with exhilaration)

Now I remember what three things always went to-

gether when I was able to see things most clearly:
three things. Three things:

(He points to where SABINA *has gone out)*

The voice of the people in their confusion and their
need. And the thought of you and the children and this
house— And—Maggie! I didn't dare ask you: my
books! They haven't been lost, have they?

MRS. ANTROBUS:

No. There are some of them right here.

*(Takes books from arm bag; gives him one—.
places other on table)*

Kind of tattered.

ANTROBUS:

Yes.—Remember, Maggie, we almost lost them once
before? And when we finally did collect a few torn
copies out of old cellars they ran in everyone's head
like a fever. They as good as rebuilt the world.

(Pauses, book in hand, and looks up)

Oh, I've never forgotten for long at a time that living
is struggle. I know that every good and excellent thing
in the world stands moment by moment on the razor-
edge of danger and must be fought for—whether it's a
field, or a home, or a country. All I ask is the chance
to build new worlds and God has always given us that
second chance, and has given us

(Opening the book)   *(LIGHT CUE #16)*

voices to guide us; and the memory of our mistakes to
warn us. Maggie, you and I must remember in peace
time all those resolves that were so clear to us in the
days of war. Maggie, we've come a long ways. We've
learned. We're learning. And the steps of our journey
are marked for us here.

*(He stands by the table turning the leaves of a
book. Steps to chair Left of table)*

Sometimes out there in the war,—standing all night on
a hill—I'd try   *(LIGHT CUE #17)*
and remember some of the words in these books.

(Sits chair)

Parts of them and phrases would come back to me. And
after a while I used to give names to the hours of the
night.

*(Hours enter from Left to platform up Center.
He sits, hunting for a passage in the book)*

Nine o'clock I used to call Spinoza. Where is it: "After
experience had taught me—"

*(The back wall has lighted up in deep blue and
reveals the shadows as they cross the platform
from Left to Right. Fred Bailey carrying his numeral has started from Left to Right. Mrs. Antrobus sits by the table sewing.)*

Bailey:
"That the common occurrences of daily life are vain
and futile; and I saw that all the objects of my desire
and fear were in themselves nothing good nor bad save
insofar as the mind was affected by them; I at length
determined to search out whether there was something
truly good and communicable to man."

*(Almost without break Hester, carrying an "X,"
starts speaking. Gladys appears at the Right door
and stands to the Right of Mrs. Antrobus.)*

Hester:
"Then tell me, O Critias, how will a man choose the
ruler that shall rule over him? Will he not choose a
man who has first established order in himself, know-
ing that any decision that has its spring from anger or
pride or vanity can be multiplied a thousand fold in its
effects upon the citizens?"

*(Hester disappears and Ivy, as eleven o'clock,
starts speaking)*

Ivy:
"This good estate of the mind possessing its object in
energy we call divine. This we mortals have occasionally and it is this energy which is pleasantest and best.
But God has it always.

*(Henry enters from down Right below set—
stands down Right)*

It is wonderful in us; but in Him how much more
wonderful."

Tremayne:
(Starts to speak)
"In the beginning, God created the Heavens and the Earth; And the Earth was waste and void; And the darkness was upon the face of the deep. And the Lord said, let there be light and there was light."

(LIGHT CUE #18)
(SOUND CUE #1)
(Sudden blackout and silence, except for the last strokes of the midnight BELL. Then just as suddenly the LIGHTS go up, (LIGHT CUE #19) and Sabina *is standing at the window, as at the opening of the play.)*

Sabina:
Oh, oh, oh. Six o'clock and the master not home yet. Pray God nothing serious has happened to him crossing the Hudson River. But I wouldn't be surprised. The whole world's at sixes and sevens, and why the house hasn't fallen down about our ears long ago is a miracle to me.
(She comes down to the footlights)
This is where you came in. We have to go on for ages and ages yet.
You go home.
The end of this play isn't written yet.
Mr. and Mrs. Antrobus! Their heads are full of plans and they're as confident as the first day they began,— and they told me to tell you: good night.

FAST CURTAIN

THE SKIN OF OUR TEETH

PROPERTY PLOT

ACT I

Floor Covering: Red carpet for step and platform of
  Pagoda—up R.

Furniture:

  1 Walnut Hamlet chair below door R.

  1 Bench, backless, red plush, cushion seat, up R.
    below Pagoda.

  1 Sofa—roll headpiece, covered in red plush,
    with breakaway legs, up C. below window.

  1 Table—round, mahogany—light in weight, C.

  1 Rocking chair—covered in red plush—R. of
    table.

  1 Armchair, mission, covered in red plush, L. of
    table.

  1 Hassock—round, covered in red plush with gold
    braid below rocking chair R.C.

  1 Side table—24 inches by 12 inches square—above
    door L.

  1 Side table—15 inches by 10 inches square—be·
    low door L.

  1 Clothes tree—mahogany—up L. corner.

Dressing:

  1 Framed picture (landscape)—"B" flat up R.

  1 Lace headpiece letttered "Mrs. Antrobus" on
    rocking chair.

  1 Lace headpiece lettered "Mr. Antrobus" on arm-
    chair.

  1 Needle point motto "God Bless Our Home" on
    Flat "A."

  1 Brass birdcage stand with wicker birdcage hang-

123

ing on spring and oversized comic stuffed
bird wired in cage—L. of sofa.
1 Pair low fireplace dogs—down C. at curtain line.
4 Short pieces wood with ends painted red—on
dogs.
1 Pair yellow rayon curtains on window up C.
1 Vase with bunch of bullrushes on table down L.
1 Lace doily on table down L.
1 Large fishbowl with comic oversized fish wired
in bowl, on table up L.

Hand Props:
1 Large bone for DINOSAUR—under sofa up C.
1 Sewing-basket with pair red wool socks—ball
red yarn, needles, darning ball—table C.
1 Large slingshot—on table C.
1 Small plate—on table C.
6 Small pieces torn paper on table C.
1 Feather duster, long handle, colored feathers—
off R. (SABINA).
1 White candlewick bedspread—off R. (MRS. AN-
TROBUS).
1 Small tin watering-can—off R. (MRS. ANTRO-
BUS).
Kitchen matches—off L. (TELEGRAPH BOY).
1 Five-pound flour bag with string handle—off L.
(ANTROBUS).
1 Package colorful wrapping with string handle—
off L. (ANTROBUS).
1 String shopping-bag with packages—off L. (AN-
TROBUS).
1 Stone wheel with center hole 28 inch diameter,
6 inches thick—off L. (ANTROBUS).
1 Railroad lantern, electrified.
1 Red plaid blanket.
2 Round trays edible sandwiches—off R. (SA-
BINA).
1 Large tray with 9 coffee mugs and spoons
(mugs painted brown inside) off R. (MRS.
ANTROBUS).
1 Pair green gloves—off R. (SABINA).
1 Pair fur-lined slippers—off R. (GLADYS).

5 Pieces of broken chair—off R. (HENRY).
1 Report card—off R. (GLADYS).
2 Pieces of broken cradle—off R. (SABINA).
1 Old guitar—1 tip cup—off R. (HOMER).
1 String bookbag with books—off R.
1 Pair thick lens eyeglasses (PROFESSOR).
1 Old brown doctor's bag—off L. (DOCTOR).
1 Stethescope (DOCTOR).
1 Old brown briefcase—off L. (JUDGE).
1 Old brown leather shopping-bag with bundles—
off L. (T. MUSE).
1 Orange box wrapped in canvas for wood-crash
effect at head of R. aisle in theatre (USHER).
2 Pieces broken theatre seat—head of R. aisle—
(USHER).
1 Large steel needle on ANTROBUS' coat lapel.
1 Key ring with bunch of keys on MRS. ANTRO-
BUS' dress.
1 Handkerchief—pocket MRS. ANTROBUS' dress.
1 Pair gold-rimmed pince nez pinned on MRS. AN-
TROBUS' dress.
1 Large triangle and beater (clock chime) off R.

ACT II

SCENE I

Furniture: 16 foot boardwalk bench with red velvet
cover—c. five feet above screen.
Hand Props.:
1 Large black leather purse with small notebook
(MRS. ANTROBUS).
1 Long piece blue silk ribbon (MRS. ANTROBUS).
1 Handkerchief (MRS. ANTROBUS).
1 Pair silver pince nez on chain (MRS. ANTROBUS).

SCENE II

Furniture:
1 Bench (same as Scene I without cover) c. two
feet above curtain.

Dressing:

    1 Stool, high with back, red—L. of Fortune Teller's Tent.

    1 Six foot ladder back of Turkish Bath flat.

    3 Standards, white ring top (orchestra pit set before Act).

    1 Thirty foot length red velvet covered rope, hook ends (orchestra pit set before Act).

    6 Standards, white ring top.

    3 Five foot lengths red velvet covered rope, hook ends—set in pairs R. of Turkish Bath; L. of Taffy stand; C. between Bingo and Fortune Teller.

    1 Pair varied colored curtains on Fortune Teller's Tent.

    24 Taffy boxes set as pyramid on Taffy Stand shelf.

    2 Large banners with wind holes on poles set in standards, red silk with gold letters—down R. and down L. banner lettered "A.H.O.M. Subdivision Humans"—R. banner lettered "600,-000 Annual Convention."

Hand Props.:

    1 Small boardwalk roller chair decorated with balloons, canes, convention favors, boardwalk prizes, etc.—down R. at rise.

    1 Small boardwalk roller chair—off L.

    1 Large boardwalk roller chair—off R.

    1 Corncob pipe, tobacco, matches (FORTUNE TELLER).

    1 Roll bills (FORTUNE TELLER).

    1 Roll bills (MONKEY CONVEENER).

    3 Cigars (CONVEENERS).

    2 Rolls bills (CONVEENERS in Bingo Parlor).

    1 Slingshot off R. (HENRY).

    1 Umbrella off R. (MRS. ANTROBUS).

    1 Large Turkish bath towel (CONVEENER in Turkish Bath).

    1 Parasol—long handle, red—Bingo Parlor (SABINA).

    1 Manuscript—off R. (FITZPATRICK).

1 Raincoat—off R. (Mrs. Antrobus).
1 Radio script—off R. (Broadcast Official).
1 Chest banner, red silk, gold letters (Assistant Broadcast Official).
2 Gingerale bottles, wrapped, off L. (Conveener).
2 Liquor bottles, wrapped, off L. (Conveener).
1 Small pill bottle with sugar pills (Mr. Antrobus).
Cigarettes and matches—Cabana (Sabina).
Varied noise-makers: horns, clackers, paper blowers, rattles, etc., off R. (Paraders).
1 Large thunder sheet—off R.

ACT III

Furniture: Same as Act I (rearranged).
Hamlet chair—down R.
Hassock—R. of trap R.C.
Sofa with foot and legs off—above trap.
Bench—up R. below pagoda.
Clothes tree leaning against door L.
Round table against base of tree and to its R.
Rocking-chair above table facing upstage.
Armchair against table and to its R.
Dressing:
Left curtain on window draped over window cross bar.
Head pieces on chairs hanging over back of chairs.
1 Fire dog standing, other down.
Firewood stacked on standing dog.
Hand Props.:
1 Hoe leaning against R. end window.
1 Sewing-basket with black sox, yarn, needles, darning ball—table.
2 Potatoes on floor at fire dogs C.
1 Prop. baby wrapped in blanket—trap (Gladys).
3 Books—trap.
1 22 Revolver in holster on belt (Sabina).
1 Flashlight (Sabina).
1 Canvas side pocket bag on shoulder strap (Sabina).

2 Large bundles wrapped in burlap—off L. (AN-
   TROBUS).
1 38 Revolver in holster to clip on (ANTROBUS).
1 Prop 38 revolver in holster on belt (HENRY).
Package cigarettes and matches (ANTROBUS).
1 Oil lamp with glass chimney (electrified).
6 Beef cubes in
1 Red silk drawstring handbag, off R. (SABINA).
4 twenty-inch square gilded boards with neck
   cords lettered in black—"IX" "X" "XI"
   "XII"—off L.
2 Manuscripts—off L. (FITZPATRICK and ASSIST-
   ANT).
1 Orange box—wood crash—off R.
1 Factory whistle—off R.
1 22 Revolver (practical) and blanks—off R.

THE SKIN OF OUR TEETH

PROPERTY CUE SHEET

ACT I

CUE #1   6 strokes of clock chime (triangle) off R.
CUE #2   Wood crash (orange box) R. theatre aisle.

ACT II

CUE #1   Thunder sheet off R.

ACT III

CUE #1   Wood crash (orange box) off R.
CUE #2   Factory whistle (2 blasts) off R.
CUE #3   Shot (22 revolver) off R.

FLYMAN CUE SHEET

ACT I

CUE #1   Screen flies.
CUE #2   Take up slack in lines on flat "A."
CUE #3   Flat "A" flies.
CUE #4   Flat "B" flies.
CUE #5   Flat "C" flies.

ACT II

CUE #1   Screen flies.

ACT III

CUE #1   Take flat "C" up one foot.
CUE #2   Take flats "A" and "B" up to position.
CUE #3   Take flat "C" up to position.
CUE #4   Prop line flies.

THE SKIN OF OUR TEETH

SOUND

ACT I

SCENE I

Front speakers on 70.
#1 Microphone on.

ACT II

SCENE I

Front speakers on 70.
#1 microphone on.
#2 microphone on 70.

#2   CUE A   Phone on 70.
Turntable #1—applause record at 33 1/3 R.P.M.
Snap up to red line then fade out.

#3   CUE B   Repeat on #1 #A.
#4   CUE C   Repeat on #1 #A.
#5   CUE D   Repeat cue #1 #A.
#6   CUE E   Repeat cue #A, while playing *snap off* A 11-12 switches #7 then fade out.

SCENE II

Right Microphone #1 on 70—stage speakers on, house speakers off

#7   #8 Left microphone #2 on 70—after Bingo call, out #1 and #2 microphones then change #1 record—put #2 record on #1 table and #3 record on #2 table—at 33 1/3 RPM—then Phone on 80 and stage speakers on 80.

#9	CUE A	Thunder—Stage speakers. #1 table outside cut up to yellow line—fade out.
#10	CUE B	Thunder—Stage speakers. #1 table up to yellow dot—fade out.
#11	CUE C	Stage speakers. Microphone #2 on 65 (2nd Bingo call) fade after call.
#12	Kill.	
#13	CUE D	***Wind*** Put in front at 63. stage and audience. Speakers on rest of Act. #2 table, outside cut up to yellow line.
#14	CUE E	***Thunder crashes***. #1 table, inside cut, up to yellow line (Maggie's whales).
#15	CUE F	Fade #1—#2 tables to yellow dots.
#16	CUE G	Fade out #1—#2 tables.
#17	CUE H	Fade up #1—#2 tables to 60 to fall of curtain.

ACT III

Table #1 at 78 RPM.
#3 record Big Ben chime.
Stage speakers at 70, set #1 table pad at red line.
CUE   Snap up microphone channel #1 to 70 for 3 strokes.

THE SKIN OF OUR TEETH

WARDROBE INVENTORY

WOMEN

SABINA

Act I: Green dress, red shoes, white petticoat, green maid's cap, pair green gloves, curl hair piece.

Act II: Red net stockings, white coat, red bathing suit.

Act III: Military cap, tan trench coat, dark blue skirt, dark blue jacket, blue shirt, pair boots, belt and holster, red dress, red drawstring handbag.

MRS. ANTROBUS

Act I: Dark red wool dress, brown shoes, stockings.

Act II: Black hat with feathers, black shoes, black purse, tan gloves, pad attached to pink undershirt, dark blue two-piece dress.

Act III: Light blue wool dress, black wool shawl, black sandals, gray hair pieces.

GLADYS

Act I: Light blue middie dress (two-piece), dark blue coat, dark blue hat, black Mary Janes shoes, black stockings.

Act II: White middie dress, white hat, white stockings, red stockings, red shoes.

Act III: Tan sandals, blue sweater, blue dress.

FORTUNE TELLER

Act II: Dark red heavy skirt, red petticoat, mustard blouse, red slippers, red scarf for turban, black shawl, bracelets, necklaces.

MISS E. MUSE
(Crying Woman Audience—Actress)

Act I· Brown dress, brown coat, brown velvet hat, brown shoes, fur neckpiece.

Acts II and III: Black dress, black hat, black shoes.

Understudy Costume: Heavy red skirt, gold blouse, red scarf, red slippers.

MISS T. MUSE

Act I: Brown dress, tan coat, brown shoes, brown hat, tan gloves, stockings.

MISS M. MUSE
Lady Conveener—Actress

Act I: Brown dress, brown shawl, black Mary Jane shoes.

Acts II and III: Blue net dress, blue straw hat, black shoes, jewelry.

DRUM MAJORETTE
Actress

Act II: Red majorette jacket, white pants, white skirt, red hat, black shoes.

Act III: Gray dress.

DRUM MAJORETTE
Asst. Stage Manager

Act II: Blue majorette jacket, white pants, white skirt, blue hat, black shoes.

Act III: Blue serge skirt, white blouse, blue coat sweater, black shoes.

HESTER

Act III: Blue broadcloth dress, apron, petticoat, sheep-lined slippers.

133

Act III: Blue smock, apron, blue coat sweater, black shoes.

MEN

MR. ANTROBUS

Act I: Two-piece brown suit, dark brown overcoat, gray fur hat, pair gray fur gloves, wide leather belt, pair overshoes, pair brown gaiters, red scarf, red blanket, 2 red and black check lumber jack shirts, blue knit tie, fleece-lined slippers, 2 mustache pieces.

Act II: Frock coat, double-breasted vest, striped trousers, fez, black gaiters, 2 white shirts—wing collars—1 tie.

Act III: Gray dressing gown, black trousers, 2 blue shirts, high black shoes, blue overcoat, belt and holster.

MR. FITZPATRICK

Acts I—II—III: Gray suit, white shirt, tie, black shoes.

DINOSAUR
(Conveener)

Act I: Dinosaur costume.
Act II: Sport shirt, black shoes, gray check trousers.

MAMMOTH
(Monkey Conveener) (Midget Actor)

Act I: Mammoth costume.
Act II: Monkey-head wig, 3-piece gray suit, black shoes.
Act III: Lounging robe.

TELEGRAPH BOY
Boy

Act I: Two-piece Postal Telegraph suit, cap, muffler, ear muffs, brown shoes.

Act II: Two-piece white suit, white shoes, shirt, tie.

HENRY

Act I: Green knicker shorts, green sweater, green windbreaker, 2 pair green stockings, high brown shoes, brown leather helmet, mittens.

Act II: Two-piece knicker suit, 2 white shirts, green tie.

Act III: Two-piece uniform suit, black high shoes, military helmet, belt and holster.

DOCTOR
Conveener—Actor

Act I: Overshoes, brown trousers, brown sheeplined coat, brown muffler, brown hat.

Act II: Striped trousers, frock coat, double-breasted vest, fez, black shoes, white shirt, wing collar, tie.

Act III: Gray suit.

PROFESSOR
Sleeping Conveener—Mr. Tremayne

Act I: Two-piece brown suit, tan overcoat, muffler, hat, shoes, gray hairpiece.

Act II: Frock coat, striped trousers, double-breasted vest, black shoes, fez, white shirt, tie.

Act III: Alpaca jacket blue vest, blue trousers, 2 white shirts, black tie, shoes.

JUDGE
Defeated Candidate—Actor

Act I: Brown trousers, brown overcoat, tan sweater, muffler, brown hat, brown shoes.

Act II: Frock coat, double-breasted vest, striped trousers, white shirt and collar, tie, fez.

HOMER
Conveener—Actor

Act I: Gray three-piece suit, shirt, tie.
Act II: Frock coat, striped trousers, **double-breasted** vest, white shirt, tie, fez, black shoes.
Act III: Dark gray overcoat, gray hat.

USHER
Conveener—Fred Bailey

Acts I and III: Two-piece light blue usher suit, white shirt, wing collar, black bow tie, black shoes.
Act II: Gray frock coat, double-breasted vest, **striped** trousers, fez, tie.

USHER
Conveener

Acts I and III: Two-piece light blue usher suit, white shirt, wing collar, black bow tie, black shoes.
Act II: Double-breasted vest, striped trousers, tie, fez.

CHAIR-PUSHER
Actor

Act II: Two-piece seersucker suit, **black shoes.**
Act III: Gray suit, white shirt, tie.

CHAIR-PUSHER
Actor

Acts II and III: Blue suit, black shoes, white shirt, tie.

BROADCAST OFFICIAL
Announcer—Conveener

Act II: Gray plaid suit, brown shoes, white shirt, tie.

ASSISTANT BROADCAST OFFICIAL
Conveener

Act II: Two-piece gray suit, double-breasted vest, chest banner, white shirt, wing collar, fez, black shoes, tie, stomach pad.

MUSICIANS

Acts I and II: 4 dark blue band coats and 4 dark blue band caps.

EXTRA ITEMS

4 Band uniform coats.
4 Band uniform caps.
1 White cape (SABINA).
1 Red majorette suit.
1 White and red cape.
1 Red majorette cap with white feather.
1 Blue majorette cap with white feather.
1 White majorette coat.
1 Green sweater (HENRY).
3 Pairs new ladies shoes (MRS. ANTROBUS)
1 Red hat with purple feather.
1 Green dress (SABINA).
2 Green aprons (SABINA).
1 Dark red wool dress (MRS. ANTROBUS)
2 Red shirts.
2 Black trousers.

SOUND EFFECT TAPE

Samuel French, Inc. can supply for $19.50 & postage.

LANTERN SLIDES

These slides are now obtainable from Samuel French, Inc. only in 35 mm. film form and can be purchased at $13.50 & postage for the set of 19.

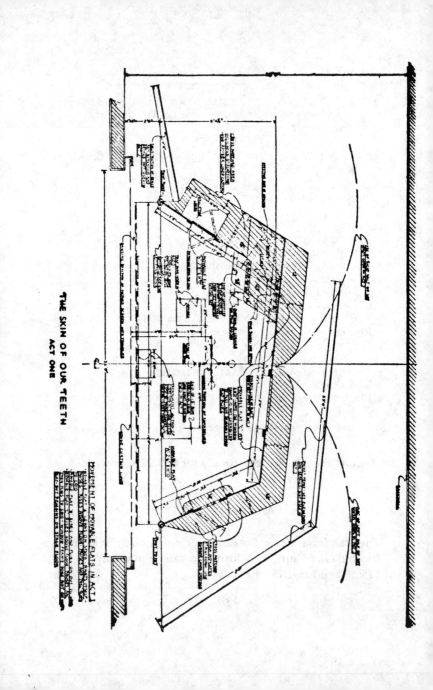

THE SKIN OF OUR TEETH
ACT ONE

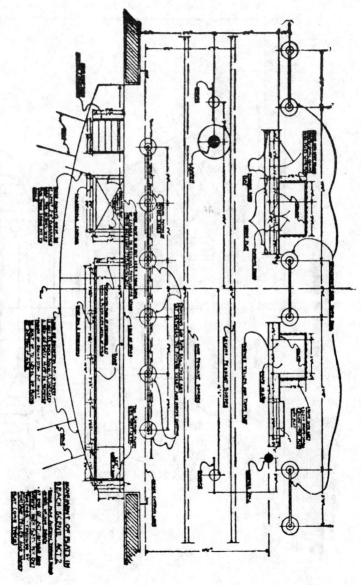

THE SKIN OF OUR TEETH
ACT TWO

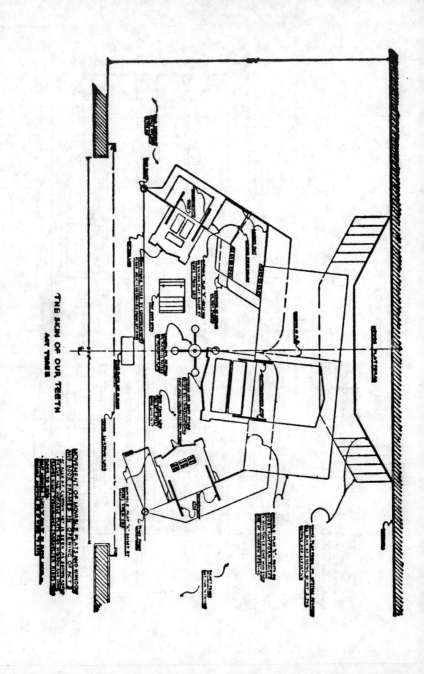